Soul Searchers

Justin Boote

Copyright © 2023 by Justin Boote All rights reserved.

No part of this book may be reproduced in any form or by any electronic or mechanical means, including information storage and retrieval systems, without written permission from the author, except for the use of brief quotations in a book review.

This is a work of fiction. Names, characters, places, and incidents either are the product of the author's imagination or are used fictitiously. Any resemblance to actual persons, living or dead, events, or locales is entirely coincidental.

Formatted by Red Cape Publishing.

Edited by Heather Ann Larson.

Chapter 1

Susanne Hill looked every bit the part with her long, wavy, brown hair that hinted at its original red when the light shone on it, her green eyes like emeralds, her pale, delicate features, and a long, flowery, kaleidoscope dress that reached her ankles. This all might have suggested an old-time hippy in other circumstances, but the cliché tarot reader was more appropriate right now. All she lacked was the black cat circling her ankles and the gold trinkets on her fingers and around her neck. Maybe a crystal ball balanced carefully in one hand while her other hand swirled over the ball insinuating mysticism and hidden secrets contained within.

Certainly, the couple who looked at her across the table wore an element of doubt on their faces, perhaps not quite believing they had let this woman in their home and what she was about to do. They kept giving each other questionable glances and flickers of a reassuring grin as all three grasped each other's hands.

"When they come through, you are not to interrupt," said Susanne. "No matter what happens, what they say through me. Normally, things will run smoothly and it will be over soon, but sometimes the spirit is reluctant to move on and the Soul Searchers have to persuade them a little harder."

More dubitative glances by the young couple suggested they weren't entirely convinced by her attempts at reassuring them. Their eyes wandered around the dimly lit room, lit by the three flickering candles on the table, as though the ghost that had been haunting them the last few weeks might make an early appearance.

"So," said the wife, Carol, "nothing bad is going to happen, is it? I mean, I've seen movies where like, another presence appears. A mean one that starts throwing stuff about and…worse."

Susanne smiled. "Movies about friendly ghosts unfortunately don't sell very well, so yeah, they embellish things, make seances seem all dark and dangerous. I can assure you I haven't ever seen anything suddenly start crawling across the ceiling or throwing people across the room. The spirits you've been seeing are just lost souls, nothing malicious about them at all. They're confused and scared and just need help moving on. That's what the Soul Searchers are for."

Her heart beat a little faster as it always did when she was forced to lie, but she wasn't going to tell them the things she had seen, the dangers she had unwittingly put others through. Nearly dying herself. This was going to be a simple operation and that was all this couple needed to know.

"Oh, good," said Carol. "I mean, nothing bad has actually happened to us or anything except by being scared witless when hearing noises in the middle of the night and seeing things. I actually feel sorry for the spirit; it always looks and sounds so sad when I've seen it clearer. I just...we wanted to be sure it will all be okay. And, well, we lost our daughter, Katie, six months ago. A...An illness. But we never once thought she might come back and visit us because we didn't believe in ghosts or the afterlife, much as we would have liked to. We just had to accept that she was gone and that was it. It couldn't be her, could it? Come back again to visit us?"

"It's very possible, yes. Sometimes spirits get lost even when they want to return to leave a message or say one final goodbye. It's obviously a very traumatic time for them having to accept they've passed away. But the Searchers will tell us. Now, shall we begin?"

Susanne closed her eyes and reached out with her mind to whom she considered her family, four spirits she had inadvertently contacted during another cleansing and who had followed her from house to house to help wayward spirits move on. Susanne had rescued them from a malevolent spirit keeping them trapped in limbo until she had forced it back to Hell. They had since bonded, deciding to stay with Susanne on what she considered her ethereal crusade to help all trapped souls reach their new destination.

As always, when she waited for them to find her, she removed all other thoughts from her head. Her body felt lighter, as though ridding itself of all excess weight and burden so she was nothing more than an empty shell, almost floating above the chair she sat upon. Her skin tingled, hair prickling on the back of her neck, as if a spider or some such creature was slowly crawling up her nape. But there was nothing creepy or scary about it; it was a soothing feeling, weightless and free from all outside troubles. She had never tried, but she was sure that if she attempted to she could astral project to the realm of the spirits or perform an out-of-body experience and join them, but it was something that had never interested her. She had the idea that if she went, visited the Soul Searchers in person, she might never return, remaining trapped just like the souls they were sent to help. And while at times it seemed quite a romantic idea, floating through the nether eternally, leaving behind this world that had caused her so much torment and pain, she also knew there were other paths she might inadvertently stumble down, roads that took one to a darker realm where nameless things dwelled. Things that were too terrifying to even contemplate let alone risk confrontation in a realm where they were master and all were slaves to their cruelty. No, Susanne was perfectly happy to remain where she was, to let the Soul Searchers do their work while she guided them, and then she could safely return to her own world in a quaint little bungalow in the small village of Bradwell.

A warmth enveloped her and the Searchers appeared before her, four vague, translucent figures like waifs or wisps of fog swirling in the darkness that made up their world. They spoke in her head, greeting her, all speaking at once and as though very far away, their words like echoes rushing towards her from some distant ravine. It might have been excitement at seeing her again or just a muddled confusion of voices, unable to control themselves anymore, but it always made her smile as she struggled to hear them speak.

"Thank you for coming again. I'm here with Mr and Mrs Durham, who want to know if the spirit in this house is Katie, their daughter. Can you see her?"

Again, a garbled response came from them, all trying to talk at once, ghostly whispers and wails reverberating in her head. Like a group of children all shouting and screaming while having fun in the playground. *Yes, we see her* was the response she understood. *And yes, it's their daughter.*

"They say they can see her and it is your daughter," she said to the Durhams, her eyes still closed, but she could feel their hands shaking as they grasped her own. A loud gasp came from them both.

"Oh my God. Katie, it's really you? We miss you so much, darling. But...but

why is she still here? Why hasn't she moved on yet? Is something wrong? Can we speak to her one last time?"

The cacophony of voices made Susanne smile as they all tried to answer her at once, and she thought she could hear another voice in the background—a young girl. *Missing Mummy and Daddy* was what the medium could make out amid the chaos. She didn't want to move on; she missed her parents.

"She says she misses you and doesn't want to leave," said Susanne.

A stifled sob came from Carol, who clutched Susanne's hand tighter. "Tell her we love her and miss her, too, but it's okay to move on. We'll see each other again soon."

Susanne relayed the message. *We'll take her*, they said. *We'll help her move along.*

She could make out the fifth spirit in the netherworld, smaller and even more difficult to see, just a tiny cloud in an infinite black, shimmering brightly. The voices in her head rose in pitch until it was impossible to hear what was being said, but slowly the five shadowy formations drifted off, like a fog heading out to sea.

"They're leaving," said Susanne. "I can see them going together now." A solitary, haunting wail echoed in her head. "Your daughter says she's going to meet with Fluffy. Does that mean anything?"

Carol sobbed again. "Oh my God. That was the name of her cat. It died a year ago. It's true then; you really can see her."

The voices fading and the sensation of weightlessness disappearing, Susanne opened her eyes and smiled.

"Yes. She'll be happy now. She can finally rest in peace."

Susanne beamed, happy another soul had been helped to move on. Yet she also felt sad as she always did in such times. There was another child up there who had long since moved on yet who Susanne still missed as much as she had the first moment they were separated. A child who caused a pang of guilt to sting her heart with the intensity of a knife wound. Would Carol's child find her, become friends with her? The Searchers had long since lost contact with her.

Susanne felt her eyes moistening and was getting up to leave before they started asking why the tearful face when a shudder rippled through her. A darkness enveloped her, making her dizzy, causing her to slump back in her chair as her eyes were forced closed again. She shivered, feeling a great weight pressing down on her body as though something wrapped her in a freezing, icy cloak or shroud. Her head swam, filled with the roaring of flames and howling of treacherous winds, a thousand wolves singing into the blizzard that now composed her mind, images flashing past her as though being swept away: souls burning alive while they screamed and wailed; creatures with a dozen limbs and mouths like caverns dashing back and forth snapping off heads; walls made of flesh that seeped thick, red blood like rusty water in a leaky basement pipe; faces peering through the walls, their eyes heavy and throbbing with gore that popped like overfilled balloons while their mouths opened wide and a million fat flies emerged, sticky with blood. And then, what Susanne knew was coming but was unable to prevent or hide from, was the infinite darkness like the universe itself reaching out for her in the shape of some hideous, demonic form, snarling and slavering like a wild beast.

Her brain shuddered with each stomp of its feet, as if it was walking directly on her skull. She was vaguely aware of voices in her ear, of being pushed and pulled, her face slapped lightly, but there was nothing the Durhams could do to help her. She willed the Searchers to come to her aid, out of desperation more than anything else because she knew they were as powerless as she was. And then, when something gripped her skull between clawed fingers and began to squeeze hard and she thought it was finally her time come to meet the Searchers in person, a voice boomed in her head. *Stay out! Or she's mine!*

Then all was silent again and Susanne's eyes fluttered open.

"Oh my God. Are you okay? What happened?" blabbered Carol.

Susanne looked around as though seeing them for the first time, wondering where she was and what she was doing in this stranger's house. But instead of answering, Susanne staggered to her feet, grabbed her coat from the back of the chair, and ran out. When she arrived home, she shut and locked all the doors and windows to her house as if the thing in her head had suddenly taken on physical form on Earth and was coming for her. She cried for almost all of what remained of the night, wishing once more she was with the person the demon had threatened her over.

Chapter 2

"Matilda! Where are you? Darren? Jane? Come out now!"

Alex Hamshore staggered around the living room, blinded with alcohol, kicking over chairs and stumbling into the wall as he searched for his family. Cheating, whinging, liars all of them, and he was going to make them pay for it. Finally. He'd had enough of their complaining and whining, sure Matilda was taking money from his wallet each night when he fell into an alcoholic slumber. Probably the kids too. There was no way he was spending that amount of money down at the pub each night, not even when the poker cards were on the table. No, they were taking advantage, knowing full well that at night not even an earthquake would wake him when he'd had too much to drink.

And then there were the two snivelling little brats, Darren and Jane. They weren't kids anymore; Darren was nearly twelve and Jane ten, acting like spoiled toddlers, their mother always mollycoddling them with hugs and kisses while he was seen as the enemy. He, the one who put food on the table and a roof over their heads, and that was how they thanked him for it? Stealing from his wallet? Hiding from him when all he wanted to do was sit them down and give them a talking to?

"Matilda! I know you're hidin' here somewhere. You come out now or I'm gonna kick your butt for you. Same for you Jane. And Darren, you show yourself like a man and take your punishment or I'll kick that greasy little smirk off your face!"

No answer. They were ignoring him again, hiding somewhere in the house because he'd locked the doors and taken the key. The windows were all closed, so they hadn't climbed out and ran; therefore, they must be upstairs. He stumbled into the hallway and tripped over the cat, which ran off screeching, crashing to his knees.

"You stupid thing!" he roared at the animal. It was Jane who had wanted the animal and her mother who had bought it for her, always caving in to her every whim. Once he'd taken care of them, he'd take care of the cat too.

Alex pulled himself to his feet, swaying while he tried to take another swig from the bottle of whiskey and cursing when the amber liquid ran down his chin. He stood at the bottom of the stairs and looked up as if expecting to see them all standing there, taunting him perhaps, but they could taunt all they liked. By the time he was finished with them, they wouldn't so much as smile ever again. Not with all their teeth missing, they wouldn't.

He placed a foot on the stairs then had to quickly grab onto the bannister to stop himself falling again. If he did, it would be their fault for making him come look for them. He supposed he could understand why they were a little reluctant to face him, and yes, he would be the first to admit that after a few drinks he sometimes got a little carried away with his hands. When he had broken Darren's leg by pushing him down the stairs that time, well, if Darren hadn't been backing away from him, took his punishment like a man, he wouldn't have suddenly reached out to grab the kid and caused him to fall. It had been an accident, happens to everyone. And as for Matilda, well, if she didn't spend all day eating sweets and watching that rubbish on TV, he wouldn't have to coerce her into doing a little more housework around the place. He was on the building site all day, sweating his butt off, while she sat around all day slouching and getting fat. Lazy pig.

A creak sounded upstairs, a floorboard stepped upon. He was right then; they were up there, probably hiding under the bed or in one of the wardrobes. Let them hear him coming up the stairs, one step at a time, one step closer to getting the beating they all deserved. He'd break their fingers, every single one of them, for stealing from him. Didn't he give her enough money to buy what they needed? Didn't the kids have the latest game consoles or mobile phones? New clothes whenever there was a new craze? Ungrateful, that's what they were.

"I know you're up there. I can smell you all. You can't run, and when I get you, you're all gonna wish you were dead."

He took another step, purposefully stomping down so they knew he was there, that he wasn't joking. He was coming for them, and they could scream all they liked—when he had stepped into the house and started roaring for them, they had been so scared they ran upstairs, leaving their phones behind. And in the middle of the night, no neighbours were going to hear them.

"Here I come, Matilda. Kids. By the time I'm finished with you three, you won't be stealing from me or anyone else ever again."

Pulling himself up, he stomped onto another step, took another swig from the bottle and smashed it against the wall, then headed upstairs to find his pathetic, thieving family.

###

"Sssh! Don't say a word. Just get under the bed and keep quiet. He'll fall asleep again before he finds us. Go on, quick!" hissed Matilda.

Her two kids visibly shook with fear, and it broke her heart seeing the tears running down their cheeks, wet patches on their trousers. She was terrified herself but knew she had to be strong for her children. She would let him take out his frustration on her if that meant he would leave the kids alone. They were innocent in all this; they had done nothing. Neither had she—it was him spending all his money down the pub then blaming his wife and kids for stealing it from him the next day when he couldn't remember anything. But this time he sounded angrier than she had ever heard him. Yes, he had hit her a few times, and there was that time with Darren, who she suspected Alex had pushed rather than her son having tripped, but he had never been this angry before, smashing furniture, throwing things around the house, roaring at them in that foul language of his. This time, his drunken rage had got out of control, and for the first time in her fifteen years of marriage, she feared for her life and that of her children.

"Here I come, Matilda!" came a roar from downstairs. She recoiled as though she had been slapped.

"Quick, under the bed and don't make a sound. I won't let him hurt you, go!"

Darren and Jane rushed over to Matilda's double bed and crept underneath like a hiding cat, their eyes gleaming in the darkness with fresh tears. Confident they wouldn't burst out crying or make a sound to give away their presence, she stepped into the wardrobe and closed the door, one hand over her mouth to stop the heavy breathing and whimpering every time he stomped onto another step. He was getting closer.

He was a completely different person when he didn't drink. He was funny, generous, and the kids loved him. They never lacked for anything, and he was always more than willing to take the kids to the beach or shopping or wherever they wanted to go on his days off work, despite being tired. And yet, as soon as he got a few drinks in him, that persona changed—a Jekyll and Hyde split personality, as different from each other as winter from summer. But usually when he came home drunk, he would shout and scream for a bit, insult everyone, then fall asleep on the sofa. Matilda had soon learned not to argue with him when drunk; it only infuriated him even more. But he had never been this bad. The things he was saying he was going to do to them, break their fingers, what kind of a father could say that to a son or daughter? She wasn't going to let that happen, though; break her fingers, but not those of her babies.

The door to the bedroom flew open, crashing against the wall, making her jump. Her hand pressed tighter against her mouth, the contents of her bladder threatening to spill free just like her children. She could hear his heavy breathing, as though the exertion of walking up the stairs had worn him out. She could smell him now too—the ripe combination of sweat and whiskey.

A floorboard creaked as he stepped further into the room. She wasn't a religious woman but prayed to God He would protect her kids, that Alex would decide to get in bed and fall asleep rather than continue looking for them. She decided in that moment that as soon as he fell asleep, she would grab her kids and they would all go to her sister's house in nearby Belton, then phone the police to get a restraining order put on him. And then file for a divorce, because it was over. She couldn't bring her children up in this environment, fearing for their lives. She should have done it years ago when he first laid a hand on her. She would get a job and things would be okay again.

She thought she heard the tiniest of whimpers coming from in the bedroom. *No, Jane. Keep quiet! Don't make a sound.* If he so much as touched her babies...

"There you are! You think you can hide from me? Think I'm stupid, is that it? Come here."

There was a scream, both a male and female howl of terror, then the sound of dragging across the carpet.

"No, Daddy, please! Don't hurt us!"

"Daddy, no. We're sorry. Ouch!"

There was a loud slapping sound like a clap of thunder followed by more screams, and Matilda forgot all about being terrified. She threw the door open and jumped out, ready to defend her kids, claw his eyes out if necessary. But the sight of him standing there with her children sprawled on the floor, red hand marks on their cheeks, and the demonic look in her husband's eyes caused her to stop. His eyes were bulging from their sockets, foam around his mouth as though suffering the onset of rabies, but what caused her soul to freeze over, for her brain to try and convince her what she was seeing was completely false, surely an illusion from a terrified mind, was the broken bottle of whiskey in his hand, shards like a monster's teeth pointed dangerously at her children. He was holding the bottle as though it was a knife.

"And there's their mother. Their stealin', lyin' moth—"

"Don't you dare touch my children," she spat. "You're drunk. Get out of my house. You so much as lay another hand on them again, I swear to God I'll tear your—"

She didn't get to finish her threat. She suddenly found herself sprawled on the floor near her kids, seeing stars, a dull, throbbing pain in her nose. Stunned, she looked down to see blood on her blouse, and when she touched her nose, her fingers came back wet and red.

"You wanna say that again?"

The imploring look of terror in her children's eyes was enough to make adrenaline race through her again. She pulled herself to her feet. "Darren, Jane, get out of here. Go. Wait for me outside. I'm coming."

They started to push themselves to their feet when Alex aimed the bottle at them. "You stay there."

He slapped Darren across the face again, and this awoke every feral impulse in Matilda's body. She ran at him screaming and snarling, fingers hooked into wicked talons. As he spun around to face her, he staggered backwards, the alcohol in his system perhaps causing him to lose his balance. Matilda jumped onto him as though giving him a welcome embrace, a boyfriend she hadn't seen in weeks, and they both tumbled to the floor. Sensing she had a temporary advantage over him, she screamed at the kids to get out while she raked at the flesh on his face.

Even though he was drunk, he was still too strong for her. Her head suddenly rocked violently backwards as he punched her under the chin, stunning her yet again, then she felt herself thrown to the side. She could vaguely hear her kids screaming something, or just screaming hysterically, she didn't know. Their father grunted and pushed himself to his feet. Her head rocked again, almost kicked off her neck as what she guessed had been his workman's boot connected with her skull. She rolled over, barely conscious but still trying to claw her way towards her husband, do whatever she could to prevent him hurting her kids.

But the kids seemed to have had enough too. They launched themselves at their father, punching him, which was as effective as being punched by a corpse. He swatted them away, but then something happened Matilda struggled to comprehend. Yes, Alex had swiped them hard across the face, but the way they both collapsed to the floor as though some massive great weight had just fallen on top of them was not normal. Then, when a small pool of blood began to collect around their bodies... No, something was very wrong here. This wasn't how they should be acting to having been slapped, and why was their urine—bladders released once again—a dark red?

It was only when she saw the broken whiskey bottle in his hand and the jagged teeth now smeared in that same dark, crimson colour, her fuddled brain connected the dots.

She croaked, her brain still unable to command movement to the rest of her body, trying to scream, to reach for her babies, yet she was incapable of anything other than a whimper, her arm reaching out feebly for them.

"Now look what you've done," growled Alex. "See, you stupid fool? You killed your own kids."

Mustering the last ounce of strength she could manage, she pulled herself upright, leaning over to help Darren and Jane, not listening to what her husband was saying; all that mattered was helping her kids. She saw the jagged, wet slash across each of their cheeks, their eyes wide and staring up at the ceiling, blood running freely down their small chests. She had to stop the flow or they were going to bleed to death, and that couldn't happen. Not to them. She flopped onto their bodies, her hands pressing hard, but the blood bubbled up through her fingers like water in a jacuzzi.

"See, I told you what would happen, didn't I?" said Alex. "See what you made me do? If you hadn't ran and hid, this wouldn't have happened. It's your own fault. You killed your own kids. How does that feel now?"

She looked up at him, the broken bottle in his hand dripping her children's blood onto her, the sneer on his face, not a care for his own son and daughter whom he had just brutally attacked. Matilda felt her features twist, crumpling into a snarling, savage beast. She pushed herself up, fingers once more hooked into claws. A scream finally broke loose as she prepared to rip his eyes out. Before she could do so, something flashed past her face, a shadowy-thing, and when the pain arrived a few seconds later across her chest, the scream became a garbled choke and she crumpled to the floor to join her unconscious son and daughter.

But their torment still wasn't over.

Chapter 3

John and Cathy Richwood grasped each other's hands and stared at the semi-detached house before them. It looked exactly like all the other homes on Sun Avenue, except the door was painted burgundy, while the others on the row of houses that stretched to its left were painted white. A three-bedroomed house with a small car park to its right, nothing striking about it at all except for that burgundy door. But what made them beam from ear to ear and for Cathy's heart to feel like it was about to explode with pride was the fact it was theirs. Not belonging to the Council like those with the white doors, but their very own; instead of paying rent money each week as they'd been doing the last five years, but a mortgage. It was the first step towards a bright and optimistic future. John said the next step would be decorating the spare room for the future baby, but that was to come later. First, get John's career firmly established in the architectural world then we'll see, as Cathy kept telling him.

John held up the keys and dangled them invitingly in Cathy's face. "You want to do the honours?" he asked.

She snatched them out of his hand then kissed him. "Of course, I insist! I've never done it before. Never owned my own place." She threw open the garden gate and ran down the path, her long, black hair tied back in a ponytail swinging left and right. John jogged to catch up to her, chuckling.

Cathy unlocked the door and turned to see John beside her, his wavy, dark hair all corkscrewed in the warm breeze blowing in their faces, his blue eyes like marbles as they gleamed in the sun.

"Go on!" he told her. "We've still got to unpack, and the cat is probably getting impatient. If he poops in my car, you can clean it up!"

Cathy giggled and threw the door open.

"Welcome to your new home," said John. "I trust everything is to your satisfaction. The cleaners came in yesterday, so it should all be good, all your demands fully complied with!"

"Idiot!" she said and playfully slapped him. She stepped inside and marvelled at how new it all looked, not a speck of dust to be seen. Considering the place had been on the market for months, she had half-expected it to be run down, full of spiderwebs in every corner, the odd window broken where kids and homeless folk had sneaked in, and the paintwork peeling. She had only seen photos of the place that John had taken when he had come from nearby Peterborough, some fifty miles away, to look at it before buying, and she had had worse-case scenario nightmares about it since.

Grasping each other's hands again, they wandered around the downstairs, Cathy delighted to see the place fully furnished, nothing required from her at all. Being an architect, John had thought of everything. Once she had a tour of the place, they went and collected the cat, which immediately began to sniff and investigate everywhere, then unloaded a few essentials from the car while they waited for the removal truck to come the next day.

"What do you think?" asked John once they'd brought in the last of the boxes.

"I love it! I still can't believe it's ours. The gardens need some work, but that's okay. And I'll have to change the curtains, of course."

"Why do women always feel the need to change the curtains once they move into somewhere new? Is this some genetic thing?"

"You could never understand. You design the homes, we furnish them. Men have no taste when it comes to home decorating."

"Yeah, well, talking of such, I have to go to the new office, meet my new boss. I shouldn't be gone long. I'll leave you to investigate all the nooks and crannies with the cat. Watch the basement—there could be all sorts of nasties crawling around down there."

"I have no intention of going down there at all, and if the cat does, I'm sure he'll kill them all for me."

"Good. That's why I hired him. I'm off. I won't be long, and I really don't want to go when we've only just arrived, but I promised I'd pop in today. Might as well do it now and get it over with."

"Yeah, go. I'll be fine. I want to start unpacking and sorting the clothes and stuff, anyway, and maybe find a supermarket or something, get some wine. We need to celebrate properly tonight," she said, giving him a wink and a slap on the backside.

"Amen to that," he replied and left, leaving Cathy alone in her new home.

Now that he was gone, she felt a little unsettled. It was too quiet, something she was used to most of the time with John working in his office at home or overseeing his latest project, but there was something about being alone in a new place she found almost intimidating, as though she was a trespasser and shouldn't be here. She went into the living room and turned on the TV just to have a little background noise, then tried to wash away the sensation by imagining what colours she might paint the walls and how she could rearrange the furniture. The sofa was directly opposite the window, so she could see people walking past, but that also meant they could look in and see her, which she didn't like either. That also got her to wondering what the new neighbours would be like; quiet and polite, or with kids that played loud music all hours of the day? The last house they had lived in, one of the kids next door had a drum kit which apparently only ever bothered her and John. The banging the kid made was so loud it made the walls tremble.

Thinking of kids, a pang of guilt stung her heart. To drown out the silence in the house, there should be the raucous, chaotic laughter of a child running about the place, checking out every little corner with the cat, bouncing up and down on his new bed, but it wasn't to be. It seemed to be the only thing lacking in their life, but John was patient, said he understood the difficulties and emotional trauma such a subject brought her, and she loved him very much for that alone. It didn't take away any of the guilt she felt, though, and she hated herself for it. For what she'd done. For lying to him.

A tear crept down her cheek as the memory of that day dared to surface. She banished it again to the dark confines of her mind, the area where all her darkest thoughts were supposedly kept under lock and key, and forced herself to think positive thoughts.

This is the first day of the rest of your life, Cathy. Your new home, for God's sake. That you own, that you don't have to go and pay rent on until the Council decides they don't want to renew the contract. This is your new home forever. Get a grip. Smile.

She did. She forced a smile to crack the dry skin, only slightly surprised to discover her cheeks were wetter than she had thought. *The sheets. Let's go change the sheets. They might be clean and new-looking, but that doesn't mean I want to sleep under them, as though we're in a hotel.* That would give her something to focus on, so she grabbed the big boxes with the bedsheets in it and carried it upstairs. Cathy dumped it unceremoniously on the floor and looked around her new bedroom. Tonight they would have a champagne celebration in bed.

At thirty-two, the dangers of encroaching years, the feared forties, celebrations were becoming less and less, Cathy feeling her age already despite how many times John insisted she was as beautiful as the day he had met her five years ago. She found herself studying her face in the mirror a little longer each night, searching for the dreaded wrinkles that would soon spring up like weeds around her eyes and corners of her mouth, checking her breasts to see if they were starting to sag yet. She told herself she was exaggerating, she was thirty-two not forty-two, but the pang of guilt she wore on her heart like a shroud seemed to spread to her outer layers as well, not just the hidden ones beneath a cloak of flesh.

Cathy looked out the window onto their back garden, the seven-foot wall giving them their cherished privacy from the neighbours next door. The cleaners might have done a great job on the inside, but the garden had been left neglected for months. Despite being summer, the rose bush looked like a skeleton in the far corner, pushing itself from its earthy tomb. The grass was now brown and withered, bald patches in some areas like the patches on John's head that had started appearing the last few months and had him, too, a little longer in the bathroom each morning as he tried to find enterprising ways to hide them.

She smiled at the thought, and his face when she occasionally teased him about it, and turned back to the bed. Thinking and reminiscing all day wasn't going to get the sheets changed. She threw them off and left them in a heap in the corner, then rummaged through the box for the new set they'd bought. She found them, pulled them out from the plastic bag they had come in, and threw one across the bed before tucking in the sides. She was about to search for new pillowcases when she heard a noise coming from downstairs.

She gasped then uttered a nervous chuckle. The cat! The poor thing, she had forgotten all about him. He had nothing to eat and no litter box prepared. He might decide to poop on the sofa or in one of the opened boxes as a show of vengeance. She had been so lost in her thoughts it hadn't occurred to her to direct him to his new kitchen/bathroom.

"Hang on, Sparky, I'm coming! Don't poop on the sofa, please!"

She hurried towards the stairs, imagining the cat with his head poking out of one of the boxes with a sly grin on his face, when she stopped. The front door was wide open. There was no way it should be open; the cat could escape and, in his confusion of being in a new home, get lost. Not to mention being hit by a car or grabbed by a dog.

She ran downstairs calling to the cat, but neither seeing nor hearing him, raced outside to the garden, looking everywhere, calling his name. When this failed to attract his attention, she ran back inside.

"Sparky! Where are you? Here, puss, puss, puss," she called, clicking her tongue.

Then she saw movement in the kitchen at the opposite end of the hallway.

"Puss!" She headed towards the kitchen, relief now replacing the terror that had been stabbing her heart, and stopped, exhaling when she saw the black cat sat in the middle of the dining room.

"There you are! You scared me, you tease! Hey, you hungry? You like your new home, with a garden to play in?"

Cathy approached her cat, who sat rigid, ignoring her completely and staring at something in the corner between the wall and ceiling. She squatted beside him.

"Hey, what is it? You see a bug or something? Spider up there? If so, kill it."

But as she tried to find whatever had the cat's interest, she realised the cat was whining in the back of his throat. His fur rose, making him appear twice as big. He hissed.

"Hey, what is it?"

She reached out to stroke his back, try and soothe him, yet as soon as she did, the cat suddenly spun around and raked his claws down her arm before sprinting off, howling upstairs. He had been so focused on whatever had drawn his attention it was as if he hadn't known she was there.

"You bad cat!" she yelped as beads of blood appeared on her arm and ran down towards her wrist. Cathy rose and peered up at the corner the cat had been glaring at but saw nothing there. Perhaps, she decided while heading to the sink to clean the wound, the spider or whatever it had been had run off. But the way the cat had been practically frozen in place, not even aware she was squatting right beside him, unnerved her. It was the first time Sparky had ever scratched her except when playing as a kitten.

And then, as she ran her arm under the tap, she turned and gasped again. One of the boxes containing their clothes was overturned, the contents strewn all over the kitchen floor. And she knew full well it hadn't been her or the cat.

Chapter 4

"No, don't go. Stay here with me. I'm scared."

Cathy crawled on top of John to stop him from getting out of bed. He laughed as she peppered him with kisses, her arms wrapped tightly around his neck.

"C'mon, Cathy. I gotta go to work. This house isn't going to pay for itself. Besides, the removal guys will be here any moment. You gonna answer the door wearing that flimsy thing?"

"Unless you stay and keep me warm for at least another hour, then yes, I will. I'll let the men in wearing nothing but this, and we'll finish the other bottle of champagne that's still in the fridge. See how you like that. They'll keep me company."

"I'm sure they will. When I went to the office to book them, I'm pretty sure the guys I saw were in their late sixties. One of them with this nice, big beer gut and most of his teeth missing. You could use his stomach as a pillow. The other one I think had rabies; he seemed to be barking a lot at the others. So sure, go for it. I think there's a mop somewhere so you can clean up all that drool afterwards."

"You pig. What if the cat attacks me again?"

When John had returned a few hours later and she told him about Sparky attacking her, he had at first been concerned, seeing the length of the gashes on her. Later, he had apparently seen a funny side to it, suggesting she should stop scaring the family pet. When she had told him about the box being kicked over, he had suggested she had been at the champagne a little early. That had earned him a well-placed slap. Eventually she had laughed about it. The cat had kept out of her way all afternoon as though conscious of what he had done.

"If you thought about feeding the cat first and sorting out its litter tray, it wouldn't want to scratch you to death, would it? It was just a little reminder. Feed me or die."

"Leave me alone in bed when I wanted to carry on where we left off last night, you might die too! So get out before I change my mind!"

John chuckled and climbed out of bed in an exaggeratedly fast way. She smiled at his lean body, still able to stay fit despite spending most of his working day sitting. *Maybe we will grow old together*, she mused. *Maybe we should think about having…*

Soul Searchers

No. Not now, Cathy. Don't do this to yourself. Focus on the house. As your husband just said, the removal guys will be here soon. If you don't move it, you'll have to answer in that skimpy outfit, after all.

"I'm gonna take a shower," he said. "It's nearly nine, you know. I think I can hear the removal van coming already."

She spread the top of the outfit she was wearing, showing her breasts. "I'm ready and waiting."

He laughed and headed off to the shower.

John was right, though, as always; it was time to get up. Groaning, she climbed out and went downstairs to make coffee and put on something more fitting. When she entered the kitchen, the cat was once again sitting in the middle of the dining room, staring up at that same corner. Conscious of the scratches on her arm, she kept her distance and looked up but yet again saw nothing. When the cat heard her, he bolted.

"What is it with you?" she muttered, making a mental note to buy bug spray when she went shopping.

Eventually, John came down, and while they drank coffee together, they discussed each other's plans. He was excited about starting his new job, which would be demanding but was what he was getting paid more money for and which meant Cathy didn't need to work, while she discussed her ideas about paint colours for the walls.

"What's our motto? I design 'em, you decorate 'em. Whatever you decide."

While she enjoyed the freedom to do as she pleased without interference, she would also have enjoyed more participation from him. It was supposed to be a joint effort decorating the new home, yet sometimes it was as though he couldn't care less. She wondered about painting the whole place black, as she had done to her bedroom as a fledgling goth teen. That would make him stop and think a bit harder.

If you gave him a child, that would help too.

Stop it.

There was a knock on the door.

"Oh, shit! Already?"

"I warned you. I gotta go. I'll leave you to it. See you tonight." John kissed her then grabbed his jacket and car keys and left through the back door, leaving Cathy to answer the front.

An hour later, the house was filled with all the stuff they had decided to bring with them, haphazardly left throughout the house because she still hadn't decided where to put everything. It was going to be a long day.

She decided the most important things should be taken care of first, and seeing as they hadn't brought much furniture with them, except those given as wedding presents, she guessed organizing the wardrobe should be the number one priority, especially given the number of boxes that contained just her clothes, never mind John's. She poured herself a mug of coffee and was heading towards the stairs when she saw the cat, now sat in front of the basement door staring incessantly at it as though it had confused the door with the front door and wanted to go and explore.

"Now what, Sparky? You're not going down there, you know."

The cat looked at her pleadingly and meowed.

"I said no. I don't know what's down there except dust and crap. I'm not having you drag spiders and bugs up here for me to find. Go play elsewhere."

She ignored the meowing cat and headed upstairs. Cathy had only been unpacking boxes ten minutes when she heard a noise coming from downstairs like a door swinging on its hinges and banging against the wall.

"Jesus, Sparky. What the hell have you knocked over now?" Muttering under her breath, she went to see what he had broken. When she reached the bottom of the stairs, she stopped, frowning. The basement door was indeed swinging back and forth, the hinges creaking like in a horror movie. The cat, though, rather than going down to explore, sat exactly where he had been before, staring into the black, cavernous pit.

"Did you open that?"

He ignored her, a low whine in the back of his throat. Cathy hadn't even bothered going down there when John gave her the first tour, convinced it would be full of dust, mould, and bugs, and the smell drifting up towards her seemed to confirm her suspicions. But she was curious and slightly nervous how the door inexplicably opened of its own accord. If the door had a habit of opening by itself, the cat could go down there to investigate and eat something that would make him ill or get trapped. The cat wasn't a kitten anymore; his days of running wild around the house were pretty much over. And he had a mild heart problem. Being stuck in the basement all night could easily lead it to be more than just mild.

She edged closer, looking for a switch and not finding it. Instead, she found long cord dangling from the ceiling, but the minute she pulled it and a dim, orange glow fought against the black, casting eerie shadows on the walls, the cat screeched and bolted up the stairs.

"Christ, Sparky, it's just a lightbulb," she yelled and chuckled, then turned back to the basement.

"Christ, it stinks down there," she muttered. "John, you've got some work to do."

From her vantage point, all she could see down there were boxes strewn about the place and general junk leaning against the walls. She coughed as another wave of mouldy air hit her, dust floating about like distant stars. She considered going down to investigate, but she had seen enough horror movies to suggest that as soon as she got halfway down, one of the steps might break and she would go tumbling down to her death, attacked and mauled by endless spiders and bugs.

"Fuck that," she mumbled, turning off the light and slamming the door shut again, ensuring it was closed properly. There was a tiny latch above the lock which she fastened and was about to go when there was a screech upstairs.

"For God's sake, Sparky! You've been here twenty-four hours already, you know. Stop freaking yourself out! Shit. Let's see what you've broken now."

She hurried up the stairs, worried he might have hurt himself, yet just as she reached the top of the stairs, the cat came bolting past her like a thing possessed and ran down the stairs howling. Despite herself, she couldn't help giggling, remembering when he was a kitten and would rush around the house for no reason at all. *Like he's got a flea up his bum*, her mother used to say.

Cathy entered her bedroom, but as soon as she put a foot inside, she gasped. The wardrobe door was wide open, but she could have sworn she saw a dark figure step into the wardrobe, the door slowly closing behind it.

"No way. Fuck this. I am not opening that door."

She considered they might have moved into a haunted house. The thought made her chuckle. Because such things didn't exist.

Chapter 5

John groaned and tried to banish the thought from his mind. One eye pried itself open, confirming what he already suspected—it was still the middle of the night. Cathy was snoring gently and muttering in her sleep beside him. The idea of having to rush to the toilet was not an enticing one.

He tried to think of different things, force his brain to focus on something else; surely, he could manage to sleep another few hours without having to get up. Because if he did get up, and no matter how quick he was, he knew from experience it would take him ages to fall asleep again. And if Sod's Law really was at work tonight, he would climb back in bed, glance at the clock beside him, and see there was only another hour before the alarm would go off. And that would be it, wouldn't it? No more sleep for John.

And he could really do with the extra couple of hours. His new job had kept him at the office later than he expected, and when he got home, Cathy had babbled on about basements and the cat and shadows and God knew what else. In the end, they had ordered Chinese takeaway because she had forgotten all about preparing anything. After that, a bottle of wine while she plied him with questions about his new job, colleagues, the colour of the walls again, and when they were going to go shopping for new curtains. By the time he stumbled up to bed, it had been well past midnight and Cathy had been all horny again.

Five minutes passed, and the urge to go to the toilet was stronger. He silently cursed the half bottle of wine he had drunk and stumbled out of bed, wincing at the frigid air coming through the open window despite it being summer. He threw on his dressing gown and hurried to the toilet, praying there was still sufficient time for him to get back to bed and get another few hours sleep.

He stumbled along the landing and almost cried out in shock when the damn cat bolted past him and ran down the stairs, almost tripping him up.

"For fuck's sake, cat," he growled. "Damn thing's gonna kill me one of these days."

He entered the bathroom and switched on the light, one hand resting on the tiled wall, already wishing he was back in bed, when he heard a noise coming from downstairs. Despite Cathy's best efforts and the relative lack of stuff they had brought from the old house, downstairs was still full of unopened boxes everywhere. The cat was no doubt having the time of his life checking out the new house while everyone slept and he had the place all to himself. That also meant knocking shit over, and John had some pretty expensive and sentimental ornaments lying about down there that would need putting somewhere when he got the time.

He groaned, seeing his precious sleep falling away like the hairs on his head as he rubbed his scalp. Was he really getting old already? His dad still had a full crop—how could this be happening to him at thirty-four? John flushed the toilet, resigning himself to the fact that his second day at his new job was going to be a very long one punctuated with multiple visits to the coffee machine, when he heard another noise downstairs. It sounded like the wind howling through an open window, yet in his bedroom there had been a chilly yet barely discernible breeze. If Cathy had left a window open and the cat got out, she would not be pleased.

Tutting, he headed downstairs to see what the cause was, mumbling expletives and rubbing the sleep from his already wakened eyes. The cat darted from the kitchen to the dining room. There was a box under the stairs next to the basement door with some if its contents lying beside it—clothes, stuff wrapped in newspaper. How the cat had managed to drag them from the box he had no idea, but he scooped them up and threw them back inside.

The wind howled again, but as he listened, wondering where it was coming from, a chill rippled up his spine that wasn't from the cold. And it wasn't the wind, either, that he was hearing coming through an open window. It sounded very much like a child crying, muffled as though with a hand over her mouth and hiding somewhere.

John strained to hear where it was coming from and exactly what it was. He thought of Cathy's childish comments about the place being haunted, and now he could understand why she might think so. It did indeed sound like something one would expect from a haunted house. He wandered around the house checking the windows, all thoughts of getting back to sleep now a distant dream. The windows were all closed, no draughts seeping through the gaps, but he could still hear it, and rather than freak him out, it was becoming pretty annoying.

Even though the wailing was distant, he could tell it was most definitely a small child crying. He pressed his ear against the wall separating him from the neighbours. Nothing. He moved towards the hallway, where the sound had been louder, and then his eyes focused on the basement. He remembered Cathy telling him the door had blown open on its own yesterday, so he figured this must be the solution. He was, after all, an architect—obviously there was a gap in the brickwork down there causing the door to blow open and causing the wailing he could hear, which was eerily similar to a girl crying. That was going to need fixing.

As an afterthought, he glanced at the clock on the kitchen wall. Just as he suspected, it was already 6:25. Another thirty minutes he would have to get up anyway. *No time like the present then.* John unlatched the little hook above the lock and opened the door. Immediately, the wailing/singing stopped. Rather than disturb him, he put it down to the draught now having a bigger outlet. He fumbled for the light cord. Straight away he was taken aback by the creepy shadows on the walls, silhouettes that flickered across the dirty, old paint like escaping beasts. He spluttered, hit by years old dust and mildew gathered down there. When he had first come look at the place a few months ago, the estate agent had been hesitant about showing him the basement when his inquisitive mind enquired about the door under the stairs, but being an architect, he had insisted. He had had visions of setting up a gym or pool table, somewhere to hide for a while if and when Cathy finally agreed on having kids. Which, since that tragic day two years ago, now seemed less likely than ever.

A cloud of regret passed over him as he thought about that, making the darkness before him even darker, if that were at all possible. He really would like to have children and thought he'd make a great dad, even though he was out of the house a lot. But evenings and weekends with a child with them, it was the missing link in what was already a perfect matrimony. If only Cathy could shrug off the ghosts of her past…

His thoughts returned to matters at hand. It wouldn't be a perfect marriage if strange noises started waking them up at all hours of the night, so carefully easing his foot onto the wooden steps, he climbed down. He didn't know who had lived here before them, but whoever it was had either died or left in a hurry. The basement was full of boxes of old junk, gardening tools, old kids toys, and rickety chairs, all leaning against one wall in particular as if the previous owners had tried to stop the wall from falling down. There was a terrible stench down here, too, perhaps a few dead mice lying about or an open wastepipe leading to the sewers. Something else he would have to fix.

There were no windows, either, which left the air stagnant and oppressive—he could practically taste the years of mould and mildew. Some kind of circulation would be required if he was going to make this his man-cave. It was cold, too, despite the lack of fresh air, as though he was wandering around some cave or mausoleum. He chuckled at the idea of a mausoleum; why the grim comparison he had no idea. Deciding there was no draft making that eerie noise, he turned to leave when something dashed past the open door at the top of the stairs. Something small and dark but too large to be the cat. He saw its shadow just beyond the door, moving back and forth as if undecided.

"Cathy? Is that you? You're up early. Why don't you put some coffee on?"

He received no reply except what he thought might be the faintest hint of whistling, like before.

"Cathy, I can see your shadow behind the door. You're not gonna scare me with your ghost stories, you know! Now, if I have to come running up the stairs and catch you, I'm gonna lock you in down here. Then we'll talk about ghosts and who's scared!"

But after a few moments, the grin on his face wavered when she failed to respond. Instead, he could hear that sound again, clearer now. It wasn't whistling, but what he'd heard the first time—a young child sobbing. Frowning, he edged towards the stairs, his head cocked, straining to hear it clearer, and slowly rose up the stairs. Whatever it was, was directly behind the basement door, the shadow still flickering now, clearly the form of a person. But just as he reached the top of the stairs, he was nearly thrown all the way back down when the door suddenly slammed in his face and the sobbing stopped. John grabbed onto the bannister to stop himself falling and threw open the door again before bursting out.

There was no one there.

He stood there for a while, looking around for the source of the ghostly wailing or the owner of the shadow, until he was forced to admit there was no one there. He laughed to himself.

"I don't believe it. Maybe Cathy is right; we're living in a haunted house! Who would have thought!"

Chapter 6

Susanne rubbed absently at the scars on her wrists. Sometimes she did so without realising, other times they itched or burned mildly, as if she had held them too close to a naked flame. That usually happened when she was troubled or thinking of past events, one in particular as if a reminder of what happened that day. As if she needed it. It was something she would take to her grave, and even then, knowing what she knew now, she didn't think it would end there. It would torment her for all eternity, whether it be in Hell, Heaven, or stuck in limbo like all the other lost souls she and the Searchers tried to reach.

She had taken her then six-year-old daughter, Sally, to the park one warm Sunday afternoon to play. Sally's father had forgotten once again to come and collect her, even though he knew damn well he was only allowed access to her twice a week, and Sally had been upset. So an afternoon at the park and then a visit to McDonald's, which Susanne hated, especially as she was a vegetarian. But the lure of McDonald's was too great to resist for a child, and Sally would resent her for life if she refused to allow her to eat there with her friends. Sally's best friend, Jenny, was at the park, so while the two kids were happily running around the park, Susanne chatted with Jenny's mother, Karen.

They had become firm friends since they both had children and lived near each other. With Sally and Jenny being in the same class together at school, developing a relationship was inevitable. Susanne always got the impression Karen regarded her as a bit weird with her long, hippy dresses, bright red hair done in complicated styles and patterns, and her openly discussing the afterlife and all things supernatural with anyone who cared to listen. *Probably thinks I'm at home all day smoking dope, listening to Pink Floyd, and that I'm danger to my daughter.* Which couldn't be further from the truth. She did listen to Pink Floyd, but she'd never so much as touched a cigarette or anything stronger in her life. When it came to the afterlife then yes, she knew an awful lot about that, since her grandmother died when Susanne was young.

Shortly after her grandmother's death, she had begun to receive visits from her grandmother while in bed at night; but rather than being scared, she had been comforted knowing Grandmother was happy elsewhere and dying wasn't the end of everything. Since then, she had devoured hundreds of books on the supernatural, so it probably wasn't too surprising others found her a little eccentric.

But later, after discovering the Soul Searchers during a private séance, she had started to receive what she could only describe as blackouts. Without warning, she would jolt, as though she'd been slapped, and her vision would go blurry. She would suffer dizzy spells, see shadows around her, grey and semi-transparent, beckoning to her. Her body would go stiff, trembling violently on occasions, and a darkness would pass over her, as though a heavy rain cloud was passing through. When that happened, she would feel the most awful sense of terror, as if her life was about to end at any second in the cruellest form imaginable. And not just hers, but everyone around her, like the apocalypse was imminent and this was the first warning. Such utter dread and dismay would cause her to scream, yet her body was so tense, so rigid, that barely a whimper would escape her tight lungs. It was also the sensation that this was caused not by some psychic reaction to her relationship with the netherworld but from something living within it, something evil and corrupt, and it was watching her, warning her not to get too close.

It happened that day at the park. Susanne was chatting happily with Karen for over an hour while the kids ran about screaming and laughing until it was time for lunch. Susanne called Sally, told her McDonald's was waiting, and together they left towards the busy main road where the fast-food chain was. And then it happened.

They were waiting to cross the road when Susanne suddenly started swaying on her feet, losing her balance. She quickly grabbed onto a nearby lamp post, the world turning grey, as though she had found herself in the middle of a thick fog. She was vaguely aware of Sally talking to her, asking if she was okay perhaps, but it was like she was calling to her from across the road. A four-avenue motorway. Figures appeared beside her, yet she was unsure if they were real people or the ghostly souls of stragglers caught in no-man's land between worlds. Regardless, it didn't matter because she let go of the lamp post for reasons she still didn't understand, stumbled, and tripped over a kerb. Then came the sound of screeching tires, people screaming, and a loud, sickening thud as something heavy hit the road hard. She knew what had happened before the world had even returned to normal and her vision cleared. And the first thing her eyes set upon was the tiny leg jutting out from underneath the white van like a broken doll and a pool of blood rapidly surrounding it.

That had been almost five years ago, and the memory of that moment was as fresh as if it had occurred five minutes ago. Two weeks later, Susanne had woken in hospital with new scars on her wrists to show off to her horrified parents and friends. It had been her best friend, Jackie, who had found her slumped in the bathtub, the cold water a dark, murky red, and Susanne unconscious, minutes away from joining her daughter. Sometimes she still resented her friend, who had since got married and moved away, for having found her and saving her life. Thanks to the Searchers, she had been able to communicate with Sally, and she knew Sally was happy and didn't blame Susanne mother for the accident. But it didn't take away an inch of any guilt she still felt, and it never would.

Her scars were sore now from so much absent scratching. She grabbed her glass of wine and took a sip, wiping the tears from her eyes. In a selfish way, she was sorry the Soul Searchers had done their job and sent Sally along; she wanted Sally to stay around forever, at least until it was her time to join her in a more natural way. But she knew she couldn't do that to her daughter. And while Sally had indeed resisted, Susanne had convinced her everything was okay, she wouldn't hurt herself again, and Sally needed to move on. That incident had also convinced Susanne that never again after saying goodbye to her would she use her abilities to contact the Searchers. Those sudden eruptions that made her lose all contact with reality and the world around her scared her badly. It made her realise the Searchers were not the only things in that realm, that there existed other, darker forces, a cosmic tug-of-war for the souls of those lost. They had warned her to back off, stay away or…

Or what?

She thought she had an idea. It wasn't the first time it had happened, and it scared her enough to cut all ties with the netherworld, until a friend came to her desperate after losing her husband to cancer. It had taken a lot of convincing, but finally Susanne had relented and there had been no sign of any dark forces, only the Soul Searchers with their manic chatter, delighted to see her again.

After visiting the Durhams the other day, it had returned. The shock at hearing that gravelly, deep voice again had been so terrifying, so unexpected, that once more she had vowed never to go there again. But leaving behind the Searchers, giving in to that demon's commands, would be a show of cowardice. She would be abandoning the spirits to their fate. And now, after thinking about it some more, she felt she owed it to Sally's spirit, her memory, to help others, not leave them by the wayside for their souls to become fodder for the darkest of all creatures.

Susanne finished her wine and lay back on the sofa, allowing all thoughts to dissipate and her body to relax. The welcoming emptiness stole the weight from her shoulders, the burdens of what made them sag, the pit of angst in her stomach. Now she was floating, astral projecting, a feather fluttering in the air. The world once more turned grey, as though lost in some immense cloud, and grey-white shadows dashed past or hovered and floated about like wisps of smoke, watching her. The Soul Searchers appeared. Immediately there was the incessant babbling and excited chatter as their formless shapes flittered about like fairies. She grinned, happy to see them again.

"No. I'm not here to help anyone along, I just wanted to see you again," she said in response to their question of what she wanted. "I missed you. Is...are you alone?"

Yes, they all said in unison. They knew who she was referring to. Maybe the demon or demons only ventured out when they sensed an unsuspecting victim, one whose soul fit whatever corrupted, perverted needs they had. But for now, she was glad they were gone.

"I'm going to continue, despite what happened the other day. The lost need me. I'm not going to let those things bully us into going away. Sally would want me to carry on."

There was a buzz of noise, like a flock of birds all singing at once, jostling to be heard. Susanne giggled, but then they quieted down suddenly as if scared or not wanting their voices to be heard.

"What is it? What's wrong?"

Be careful, said a single voice, almost in what might have been a whisper. *Sally is happy for you, but you have to be very careful. You are about to get involved in something that could destroy you. You and all your loved ones. Please be very careful. There is great danger heading your way.*

And with that they were gone, as though they had scared themselves with their message. Susanne opened her eyes, the sagging weight returning to her shoulders, and poured herself another glass of wine, confused. The glass shook in her trembling hand.

Chapter 7

"Oh my God, you're kidding!" exclaimed Cathy. "Really?"

"I'm telling you, I thought it was you trying to scare me or something. There was this sound that I assumed was the cat having knocked something over again, so I went to check, and there was a box with stuff all pulled out. Couldn't have been the cat, but I was half asleep anyway. Then I heard what I thought was whistling, like a draught. Went through the house and it was louder in the basement, so I went down, was about to come up again, and that's when I saw the shadow behind the door, moving backwards and forwards. Then the door slammed in my face, nearly broke my nose. I opened it and there was nothing there and you were still in bed."

John took a long sip of his coffee, grinning at Cathy. She laughed seeing him sitting there with his corkscrew hair and gleaming eyes as though he had just discovered a dirty secret.

"You don't…I mean, I don't really believe in all that crap, but…Do you think the house is haunted? That would explain why the place has been empty for so long and was cheaper. It sounds so cliché, like a crappy horror movie, but…"

John sat and thought for a moment, eyeing Cathy as though considering she might be mad. She felt slightly mad for suggesting the idea, but if he was telling the truth, and there was no reason to hint he wasn't, then on top of what she had seen and heard, it would all make sense. And yet, *ghosts*?

"I don't know. It could be that we just moved in and haven't acclimatised yet. Houses make all kinds of weird noises sometimes, you just get used to it, so moving into a new one…Draughts, shadows that you're not used to seeing. I should know, I'm an architect. I'm trained to prevent these things from happening in new buildings, but in older ones like this, it happens all the time."

"But what about the box? There's no way the cat knocked it off or tipped all the stuff out—it was too heavy and too full for him to climb inside. And I've seen him staring at things, getting spooked. Hell, look at the scratches on my arm. Sparky has *never* scratched me before."

"Yeah, well, again, new house, cat freaks itself out. The box, I don't know. Maybe it was already knocked over and we just didn't notice, but I don't think so. I'm sure I would have seen it before. There was some valuable stuff in there. It's just...*ghosts*? A *haunted house*?"

Cathy could tell from the look in his eyes, the way he chewed his bottom lip, he was definitely considering the idea despite trying to convince both of them it was nothing but draughts and funny shadows. The cat was definitely unhappy and spooked here; he spent most of his time staring up at the corner in the dining room or sat in front of the basement door as if waiting for something. Or someone. And would then proceed to bolt screeching up the stairs to hide under the bed in the spare bedroom. And while both of them enjoyed watching the occasional horror movie, the few times they had discussed the possibility of there being an afterlife both had dismissed such a concept. As John had pointed out, they were in the twenty-first century and there wasn't a single, defining piece of evidence suggesting it was so, no proof of the afterlife. With everything science was capable of nowadays, it seemed highly unlikely they hadn't figured it out yet. But as far as she was concerned, facts were facts, and *something* weird was happening here.

"I must admit, though," continued John, "it did freak me out a bit. That door slamming in my face. And I would swear it was a little girl crying or something. I know the difference between crying and the wind whistling through a crack in the brickwork or window frame. It's just..."

"It's romantic, that's what it is! We're living in a haunted house. We should throw a party. A housewarming party with the new neighbours and stuff. Maybe they'll tell us the house's history."

"Woah, hang on. You want to throw a house-warming party then tell everyone it's haunted? They'll drive us out of town, think we're mad or eccentric. That famous mental hospital is not far from here—Northgate Hospital for the Mentally Impaired. You wanna spend five years stuck in there being spoon-fed all sorts of weird medication? Because I don't. I've only just started a new job—I'll be sacked before I even got comfortable in my new chair."

"It'll be fun! We need to meet the neighbours anyway. This is our second day and we haven't even said hello to them yet. They'll think we're weird just for that. Like we're in some secret cult or something, or antisocial."

"Okay, that part I can understand. Although they haven't exactly rolled out a welcome mat for us either! I need to get ready for work, anyway; I'm already late. I'll leave it to you then to organise, but perhaps get all the boxes put away first?"

Cathy gave a little yelp of joy and hugged him, almost knocking the coffee mug out of his hands. This was going to be fun. Were they going to discover there had been a brutal series of murders, a few suicides, perhaps? Ghosts didn't harm people for real, not like in the movies. Besides, it would give her something to do. There was also the issue of the guilt that tortured her soul after what she did two years ago—maybe the little thing hadn't completely died, after all.

Chapter 8

It turned out the neighbours next door did have a son, but he was only eight and had yet to discover the joys of hitting pieces of canvas as hard as he could with a set of drumsticks. The Rashfords, Dave and Carrie, were a little older than Cathy and John, and both seemed a pleasant enough couple after Cathy knocked on their door and introduced herself. She was invited in for coffee and told them they had just moved from Peterborough to be closer to John's new firm and had been so busy they hadn't had time to introduce themselves earlier. Carrie was a stay-at-home mum with Peter, their son, and Dave worked for the bank. Cathy broke the ice by suggesting that at least with times as they were, they didn't have to worry about being denied a loan any time soon, which they all laughed about.

But all the time they were exchanging pleasantries, there was only one topic on Cathy's mind, one thing she was dying to ask them about.

Who lived in the house before us? Have you ever heard of anything...weird happening in there? Did anyone die there? Is it haunted?

She had to bite her tongue to stop herself from blurting out the questions, worried the answer to all of them may be in the negative and they would think the Richwoods were perhaps a little strange and best avoided. She decided she would bring up the subject discreetly, tactfully, if they agreed to come to her housewarming party, but they could at least answer one question which may give her an idea of where to start looking for answers.

"Who lived in the house before we moved in? Whoever it was kept it very well maintained. We hardly had to do anything. I'm going to paint it anyway, but it doesn't even need that."

There it was, that tell-tale glance between Dave and Carrie, barely perceptible. If Cathy had blinked at just that moment, she would have missed it. There was also that hesitant pause between them. *Are you going to tell her or shall I?* Carrie provided a weak smile. Cathy could almost see the cogs in her brain grinding together, trying to figure out a suitable response without scaring off her new neighbour. *Well, as it happens, there was a big family that lived there just before you did, but something happened. It's strange because they were always such a nice family, but then one day the husband came home and killed them all with an axe. Took their heads right off, he did. Isn't that sad? No one's lasted more than a few weeks in that place since.*

"Well, there was a family that lived there before, with their two children."

See, told you.

"But I believe they divorced and all went their separate ways because we didn't see them again. They left quite suddenly it seemed; one day they were there, and the next it was empty. But I've seen the estate agent pop in and out quite a few times, and then they had the cleaners and some workmen come in to tidy it up again. But why it's been empty for so long I don't know.

"It's nice to finally have some new neighbours, though—the couple next to us are rather quiet and keep to themselves," she added after a moment's hesitation.

That last sentence seemed rather forced, but Cathy let it pass. That comment about the family suddenly up and leaving had her intrigued, though—definitely something to look into later when she was alone on her laptop. So, without mentioning anything about possible ghosts and haunted houses, she told them they were having a little housewarming party and all three were invited. The half-smiles of acceptance on Carrie's and Dave's faces did not suggest they were entirely thrilled at the prospect.

Cathy and John had no family within a reasonable distance, so John invited his boss and his wife to come along so it wasn't too small a party. When Cathy knocked on the doors along their row, all declined with various excuses. So the next night it was six adults and one child, Peter, at the welcoming party.

It was quiet at first, no one knowing the other well enough to know what to talk about, so most of the chatter revolved around the best restaurants in Bradwell, a few of the funnier stories of things that had happened in the area, and the most popular subjects—the weather and politics.

Cathy was pleasantly surprised to see John's boss was a funny man, constantly telling them all jokes and stories of some of the greatest architectural disasters he knew of. But really, she wasn't that interested. She wanted to know about the previous owners. She wanted to discuss the possibilities of ghosts existing. She wanted to know if anyone sensed anything odd about the place, a weird vibe, anything, but no matter how glued to their expressions she remained, no one acted the slightest on edge. Except Peter, who had long since got bored with adult conversation and had wandered off by himself to apparently torment and play with the cat. Peter's parents, it seemed, had forgotten he was even there.

###

Peter had always wanted a pet, but for some reason his parents wouldn't let him have one. The only thing resembling a pet he had ever had was a gerbil when he was five, but the novelty of that had soon worn off. He wanted a cat, something he could play with and that would sleep with him in bed at nights, keeping him company; yet no matter how much he begged, how hard he pleaded whenever Christmas or his birthday came around, he got the same response. "Maybe when you're older, Pete."

Well, now he was older, eight, almost nine, and still they refused. So when he saw the new neighbours' cat dart past as he sat bored with his parents, he ran off to find it, delighted. He thought he had seen it dash upstairs, but as he checked each room, conscious he might get in trouble for going in the neighbours' private rooms even though they had given a tour of the place, he called for it but couldn't find it anywhere. He looked under the beds in what the neighbours had said were the spare bedrooms, then went into the main bedroom.

"Hey, puss! Psst! Psst! Psst! Where are you?"

The cat wasn't under the bed, even though he was pretty sure he had heard a noise as he debated whether to step in or not. He crawled out from under the bed and stood up, wondering where else to look, when he heard another noise coming from behind. He spun around to see the large wardrobe doors were slowly swinging open.

"There you are! Found you!"

Grinning, he threw the doors opened wider and peered in, rummaging around boxes and pairs of shoes on the floor.

"Hey, cat. I saw you come in. Where are you?"

He crawled in further, pushing aside the neighbours' clothes until he was completely inside the wardrobe, yet he couldn't understand why he hadn't found the cat yet. The wardrobe wasn't *that* big. And then everything went black when the doors suddenly slammed closed, making him jump. Within seconds of each other, two completely separate emotions threatened to smother him like the dark in the wardrobe. First, the inklings of a grin that this might be part of a game, his parents or the neighbours slamming the doors shut and at any second someone would open them and yell *gotcha* at him. But that was soon replaced by the unnerving possibility he was now locked in here forever. It was a game, but something—the wind perhaps—had slammed the doors on him and he was going to starve in here. Unless there was something in the wardrobe with him that might be hungry itself.

The beginnings of the smile he had been wearing rapidly faded as he searched for a handle, but of course, why would there be handles on the inside of a wardrobe? He pushed at the doors, threw his shoulder at them, and when they still refused to open, a sob caught in his throat and his intestines suddenly felt like live snakes squirming away in there. Pete banged harder and began yelling, certain the loud thuds would be heard by the adults downstairs, but what if they weren't? After a while, they would come looking for him, but how long until then? The utter pitch black in here was scaring him. What was probably a sleeve from some jacket was now very possibly a hand brushing his shoulder. Whatever was tickling the top of his head—surely a coat hanger—might be a bony finger ready to pluck his eyeballs out. His yells for help turned into screams of desperation. One last push at the doors and they swung open, and he fell into the bedroom, crashing to the floor in his exertion.

The cat was sitting directly in front of him. It gave a yelp of surprise and darted off. Freed from his dark prison, seeing the cat dash off like that took away all his incoming terror. He felt a little foolish for the panic that had threatened to overwhelm him. He was almost nine, far too old to be getting scared that easily anymore. So, slightly embarrassed, he banished the incident from his mind, jumped up, and ran off once again in search of the elusive feline.

He found it sitting at the entrance to the basement, the door wide open. His parents and the neighbours were laughing at something someone had said. Peter approached it slowly, not wanting it to run off again, but even as he squatted and stroked it, it arched its back and glared at him briefly, as if it hadn't even been aware he was there.

"Hi, puss. What you looking at? Something interesting down there?"

He peered down into the gloomy basement, momentarily remembering what happened in the wardrobe and deciding he was most definitely not going through all that again, when he heard what he thought was another cat meowing down there. Again, conflicting emotions rumbled in his brain. He really didn't want to go down there, it had to be full of spiders and bugs, and it was so dark. But what if the cat was hurt or something? He thought of telling the neighbours, but they were all laughing and joking in there, and his mum might decide it was time to go home. He didn't want to; he wanted to play with the cat for longer now that he had him.

First things first, then. He stood up and fumbled for a light switch, almost jumping back when his hand came upon something dangling from the ceiling. He pulled it and the basement lit up, albeit still gloomy and looking like his suspicions of bugs may prove correct. The meowing sound came again, pitiful and weak, and unable to resist, Peter slowly walked down the steps, calling out to the surely-injured animal.

He reached the bottom of the stairs and looked around, making clicking noises with his tongue. When he turned around, the other cat was still sitting at the entrance, staring down at him, its eyes like bright stars in the reflection of the lightbulb. Something shifted behind him, then he heard a scratching sound like the cat was sharpening its claws.

"Puss? Where are you?"

There was a bunch of junk against one wall, so he headed over to it, squatting as he searched for the other cat. He pulled aside a small bicycle and yelped when two eyes peered back at him then abruptly disappeared. He gave a nervous chuckle, stood up, and continued looking. The scratching sound continued, but as he strained to hear it, it sounded like it was coming from behind the wall he was staring at. He pushed aside a box and pressed his ear against the brick wall. Yes, it was definitely coming from behind there. Confused, he assumed there must be rats behind it or something, but that didn't explain the meowing. Then he realised. Obviously, the cat had come down here snooping about and had heard the rats so had found a gap in the wall and now probably couldn't get out.

He crouched down again, feeling for any holes in the wall and calling to the animal when three loud thumps came from the other side of the wall. He jumped back, banging his head on a piece of furniture. The banging came again, down near the floor, then suddenly from the top near the ceiling. And then the whole wall came alive with the sound of pounding thumps, the wall rattling, bits of brick and dust falling onto his hair. And now what he heard wasn't a poor cat lost and stuck behind a wall but wailing, endless screaming and howling that made him cover his ears and scream for help. Something tugged at the back of his t-shirt, pulling him out from behind the boxes. Peter was thrown onto the floor, sprawled out as though he had been kicked, while the incessant howling and screeching continued. The thudding on the wall was so loud he was sure it was going to come crashing down on top of him.

He tried to push himself away, his legs jelly, refusing to cooperate, and he yelled for his parents to come and save him. When he managed to turn his back to the wall, pushing himself towards the stairs, a shadow dashed past. A small figure clad all in white, the dress she was wearing smeared and covered in some dark, red substance, ran behind an old bookcase, then stopped and peered out at him from behind it. Her eyes were golden like flames, her skin a mottled grey colour inflicted with deep gashes and bruises, bone from her cheekbones jutting through the cracked flesh. Then, when an arm reached out and pointed at him accusingly, he found his strength and bolted up the stairs, screaming hysterically for his parents. The door slammed shut behind him, narrowly missing the back of his head, the cat watching him with apparent interest as he burst into the living room, sobbing wildly.

Chapter 9

Susanne finished serving a customer in the small shop she ran when the phone rang. She set up the business some three years earlier, selling what one passer-by claimed to be 'hippy shit.'—incense, tarot cards, books on the afterlife and self-help guides, dealing with grief, anything and everything related to the paranormal and white magic.

She also did private tarot readings in the back, with her cliché candles dotted about the room and soft, ambient music in the background, helping others in reaching out to deceased friends and loved ones. She always told them there were no guarantees and never charged anyone if contact was not made, but nine times out of ten, her intentions seemed so sincere to the clients they insisted she accept payment anyway.

It all went towards financing her retirement dream—a nice little cottage complete with thatched roof typical of English country villages. There were a few dotted around the area, and she hoped in maybe ten years she could retire already and dedicate her free time to working with the Soul Searchers and paying her bills doing readings. She didn't know if it would work out that way, but it was a nice dream to have, one that kept her focused on moving forward and not allowing distant, dark memories to resurface. Sally would be proud of her.

Susanne answered the phone greeted by a lady who seemed to be in some distress. She said her mother had recently passed away and she wanted to reach out to her, tell her she loved her, and ask her forgiveness for something that had happened between them.

"But…you're not a scammer, are you? I mean, I got your name from a friend who said you really helped her out in a similar sort of thing, but well, my friend is a bit naïve. She's easily fooled. I'm sorry if I sound a bit blunt, but it's very important to me."

Susanne smiled. It was something she was used to. She had been called a lot worse than scammer in her time, and she knew that yes, in this day and age with science and technology finding answers to everything, it still seemed difficult for some to believe in the possibilities of an afterlife. Or even in God.

"I do my very best to help others find their loved ones again. I don't charge anything for it, it's just an ability I was blessed with, and

I like to use to try and reunite people. I've been in that situation before, so believe me, I know it can be a difficult subject. Just give me your address and I can come by tomorrow."

"Really? Oh, thank you so much. I did try one person before, but he wanted to charge me money whether he succeeded or not. My husband refused to do so. There are so many tricksters and cruel people out there waiting to take advantage of others."

Susanne reassured her no payment would be expected of her and that she couldn't guarantee anything, either. The woman gave her address and they agreed to meet later that day. When she hung up, she was smiling. Both for the woman having confidence in her to try and contact a loved one and mainly for herself; just a few days ago, she had been on the verge of giving up, too scared to confront whatever nightmares lurked in the netherworld.

Susanne arrived at the Morgans' home shortly after closing the shop. As always, she stood outside the house first, looking up into the windows, trying to ascertain any sensations of feelings emanating from the place. Sometimes she felt like the priest standing outside Regan's house from *The Exorcist*, the popular cover from the novel, trying to garner enough courage to walk down the garden path. She never knew what to expect from these visits: utter delight and relief from her client or, like the other day, a darkness enshrouding them all with dire warnings to get out and never return. But she had convinced herself that if the demon wanted her to keep away, surely it must fear her. That was a good thing, right?

Sensing nothing out of the ordinary, Susanne climbed the steps and knocked on the door. It was opened by a middle-aged woman who, not recognizing Susanne at first, eyed her with mistrust.

"I'm Susanne Hill. We spoke on the phone earlier. You must be Agatha."

The woman's expression changed instantly to welcoming, a broad smile on her too-pallid features. There were dark bags under her brown eyes, as though she hadn't been sleeping well lately. Nothing Susanne hadn't seen too many times already.

"Oh, hi! Yes, of course, please come in!"

Agatha stepped aside and allowed her in.

"I'm sorry, I haven't been sleeping well lately. This whole thing has been worrying my husband and me immensely. I do hope you can help."

"I'll do my best," said Susanne, surveying her surroundings.

Agatha took her to the living room, where her husband was slouched on the sofa watching TV. "This is Dennis, my husband. Dennis, this is Susanne, come to help us contact my mother."

Dennis rose from the sofa to greet her, wariness in his eyes too. "Nice to meet you. I sure hope you can help us out here. Even in death my mother-in-law haunts us."

Agatha chuckled nervously.

"I'll do my best. So, what exactly has been happening?"

They exchanged nervous glances while Susanne sat at the table.

"Well," said Agatha, "as you've probably guessed, my mother. She lived with us after being diagnosed with cancer, and well, because of the pain she was in, she could get quite upset, often snapping at us both for no reason. I know it wasn't her fault, but things could get quite tough around here. She started losing her mind, saying horrible things, but it wasn't really her saying it—it was the morphine and all the drugs she was on. Half the time she didn't even know who we were.

"And then a few weeks ago she died. I was relieved more than anything—she was suffering so much. But a few days later, well, things started happening. We'd come home from work to find pieces of furniture moved about. I'd lose my keys then find them in the strangest of places. In the middle of the night we'd hear banging on the walls, doors opening and closing by themselves. Then one night Dennis got up to go to the toilet and saw someone standing at the bottom of the stairs, yet as soon as he flicked the lights on, the person disappeared. I'd start to smell the perfume my mother used to use all the time, really strong, especially in the spare bedroom where she died. The spare sheets would be all ruffled as though someone had been asleep there. And then I started seeing her myself. I'd be in the kitchen preparing lunch and would feel eyes on the back of my neck. When I turned around, she'd be standing there, looking…awful. Her skin all grey and peeling. Her eyes bloodshot. Then, as I stood there, shocked, she'd let out this terrible, deafening scream and disappear. It happened a few times, like she was trying to scare us on purpose, but I have no idea why. I just want her to move on. Or if there's something she's trying to say, to tell us and go."

This was strange. If Agatha's mother had been in so much pain, she should have been relieved to finally move on, not hang around in limbo tormenting everyone. Susanne had an idea that perhaps Agatha wasn't being too honest with her. Ghosts only hung around when they had unfinished business that needed resolving, a wrong needed righting, or they desperately missed someone and didn't want to leave them behind. She didn't think that was the case here unless she wanted to apologise for her behaviour while sick. But she could have done that quite easily without scaring them in the process.

Susanne told Agatha it was unusual, but she would do her best to contact her, discover the source of her unhappiness. They joined Susanne at the table in the living room after Dennis turned off the TV and closed the curtains. There were two candles in the middle of the table to give them enough light to see with.

With Dennis to her left and Agatha to her right, she told them to hold hands to form a bond between them. As always, a nervousness rippled through Susanne's body, in this case more so. Agatha was keeping something back. Susanne allowed her mind and body to loosen, remove all the weight and tension from it, like unloading a lorry, until the familiar floating sensation took over. The Searchers buzzed and flitted as soon as she made contact.

"Hello again, friends! Are you alone up there?"

They knew what she meant, but Susanne didn't want to worry the Morgans—they looked worried enough as it was.

Yes, we're alone. How can we help you?

"I'm looking for Vera Morgan. She died recently and is still hanging around. Can you find her?"

As usual, a multitude of wispy, grey shapes floated or sped around the vast space. It never ceased to amaze Susanne. A world bigger than the universe, infinite and desolate at the same time, many of the souls trapped up there sorrowful and desperate to leave even though it seemed such a peaceful world. But she knew better.

Yes, we see her. But... There was a cacophony of whispers and hissed muttering, like excited children all talking at once when they weren't supposed to.

"But what?"

Her aura is dark. She's troubled, angry. She doesn't want to leave. She says she has unfinished business. She wants to make them pay for her suffering.

Damn. She knew it. An angry spirit was always the most difficult to move on. The most stubborn. Agatha and Dennis were surely responsible in some way for whatever grieved Vera. Now she had to consider her words, not alert Agatha and Dennis something was wrong. An angry spirit could be troublesome in more ways than one.

"Tell her Agatha wants her to move on, she's been scaring them recently. She needs to move and finally rest in peace. She deserves to, her daughter says."

More manic clamouring and commotion followed. The room darkened, the candles flickering despite all windows being closed. Although Susanne's eyes were closed, she sensed another presence in the room with them. Eyes were burning into the back of her head. Warm, putrid breath filled her nostrils.

She won't. She refuses, says her daughter has to suffer as much as she did. That's why she won't move on. They caused her great suffering.

Susanne noticed Agatha's hand grip her own tighter. She was also aware of something else there with them. Agatha's breathing was harsher, faster, yet no sound came from Dennis.

"Susanne? What's going on? What are they saying?"

Susanne frowned. They were not supposed to interrupt her while she was away; it broke her concentration and made that other world flicker and fade, like the picture on an old TV screen.

"Tell her she needs to move on. It's not good for her or anyone that she remain behind," insisted Susanne.

She watched as a hazy, darker shadow flitted between the Soul Searchers—Vera's aura blacker than the others, a sign of her indignation. The Searchers surrounded the spirit, trying to lead her to another place, but she could tell Vera was refusing. Her image was jerky as she flashed around them, like a puppet on strings guided by amateur hands.

Something brushed Susanne's hair. Something cold and clammy ran gently down her back, like a knife or claw tracing an outline of where the first incision would be made.

"Agathaaaa," was whispered in Susanne's ear, barely discernible but enough to trigger another ripple of fear to course through her body.

"She hurt me. She hurt me so much. Did bad things. Painful things. So much torment. She needs to pay."

As soon as Vera finished there was a loud bang in the room, forcing Susanne to open her eyes in her shock. The spare chair beside her lay on its back on the other side of the room. A photo of a smiling Agatha with her mother when they were much younger toppled from atop the television and smashed onto the overturned chair. Susanne turned to Dennis and Agatha. Their eyes were wide with terror, their jaws dropped, bottom lips trembling.

"You see?" said Agatha. "What does she want? Why won't she leave us alone?" she practically wailed.

"What happened to her really, Agatha? There's something you're not telling me. I don't mind either way, but I can't help her if I don't know why she won't move on. She says you caused her a lot of suffering and she wants you to know that."

Agatha's hand rose to her mouth as she gasped. "But...but that's not true. We did everything to make life easier for her. It wasn't my fault she got cancer. We—"

"That's not true, is it?" interrupted Dennis. "And you know it." He turned to Susanne. "When she came to live with us, she was already in advanced stages, and...well, to be honest, she was never the nicest person you could ever meet. She once told me that she wished she'd never had Agatha. That she ruined her youth. She wanted to have an abortion, but her own mother wouldn't let her, and it seems she was damn determined to make her—both of us now—pay for it. She'd soil herself on purpose, throw her food at the wall, wake us up constantly in the middle of the night for the most stupid of things. So...sometimes our patience got the better of us. If she was going to throw her food on the floor, sometimes we stopped feeding her. As soon as we changed her after soiling herself, she'd strain to do it again, so yeah, sometimes we left her like it all day and night. It hurt us both to do it, but this went on for months. We just couldn't cope anymore, and she refused to go to a nursing home. It sounds terrible, but we should have put her out of her misery—all of our misery—much earlier."

Agatha stared at her husband, dumbfounded, but neither denied nor confirmed what he just said. Susanne simply nodded. At least she knew Vera's reasons for staying behind. She wanted revenge even after death for having an unwanted child. It didn't make Susanne's job any easier though.

"Okay. I'm not here to judge, just to do a job. Now, we need to start again. Don't interrupt me or the connection will be lost again. Next time, possibly for good."

Soul Searchers

Susanne closed her eyes and clutched their hands, forcing herself to breathe calmly, ignore the sensation there was still someone in the room with them, someone with a vengeance, an air of negativity she could still smell, floating in the air like the remnant of a bad dream.

"I'm back. Tell Vera they're sorry for what they did. They apologise and wish none of this had ever happened. That Agatha is sorry Vera never wanted to have children but she must move on. It's not good for her or anyone."

But the Soul Searchers were strangely silent. Their shadows, instead of flitting about like boisterous children, were alarmingly still. None of them replied to her. Susanne searched for Vera's spirit, but now there was a shadow hanging over that world far too big to be Vera's. The house seemed to shudder on its foundations, as if scared by that otherworldly presence. The floor beneath her shook, as though earthquakes had suddenly found their way to eastern England. But this was irrelevant compared to the shadow looming over her in the other world she currently inhabited.

The Soul Searchers were silent, not daring to move or speak. With each pounding thud that shook this world, it was as if the approaching creature was stepping directly on her skull, crushing it slowly under the weight. A sense of utter despair and horror crippled Susanne's mind, unable to escape the onslaught of terror. The shadow partially revealed itself to her, a multitude of limbs like tentacles swirling in the netherworld that now resembled a thick fog, the spirits within lost as they mingled in the cloudy substance. A face appeared, nothing more than huge, gaping teeth, cannibalistic and razor-sharp, that jutted down past its chin. Up above, its nostrils flared. There was another, much smaller shadow beside it, less fearful, yet in its own way just as terrifying.

Vera.

She had decided not to listen to her daughter or the Soul Searchers, instead wanting to feed a more feral desire—revenge. The house continued shaking. The bond between Susanne and the Morgans was broken as they screamed and jumped up, covering their heads with their arms as though the house was about to collapse upon them.

I said to stay away! You didn't listen. Now she's mine for all eternity, as is your daughter. I will pluck her from her grave and bring her back to be at my side. Your world from now on will be nothing but cruelty and suffering.

As if to prove his point, she was thrown back into her normal world, although there was nothing normal about what suddenly happened. The table she was sitting at wobbled and rose into the air before being hurled against the wall by invisible hands, smashing on impact. Cracks like scars appeared on the windows, while the curtains flapped and flew across the room like ghosts. The windows imploded, showering everyone with sharp fragments. The chairs shot to the ceiling, dangling there like some magician's trick, until they shattered too. Dennis and Agatha screamed, tried to run from the room, but the door slammed in their faces with such force the plaster on the walls cracked.

"Leave us alone!" screamed Susanne, cowering in a corner, trying to avoid being killed by flying furniture. There was a huge bang, as if a bomb had exploded upstairs, causing the house to visibly shake. Then the whole house went silent save for the desperate panting and sobs from Agatha and Dennis. All three of them remained in their cowered positions, not daring to move, for several long minutes until they dared to stand up again. Dennis and Agatha stared at Susanne as though she had been responsible for what just happened.

"What did you do?" sobbed Agatha. "What the fuck did you do? Get out!"

Susanne didn't bother arguing. She grabbed her purse and ran from what looked like a war zone.

Chapter 10

John had already left for work by the time Cathy woke. She stretched, saw the sun beaming at her through the open window, and smiled. Another gorgeous day, it seemed, not a cloud in sight, perfect for pottering about in the garden ripping up weeds then head into town for some seeds to plant. Then hang the new curtains. Now that they had been here a few days she figured she could let the cat out with her in the back garden as well. She knew cats liked to take their time to prowl and investigate their new surroundings, but Sparky had been acting weird ever since they moved in.

Before, he had claimed one side of their bed as his own and would head up every night without fail for a nap, often ruining a little lovemaking session, scratching at the door incessantly to be let in until they relented. Now he refused to even come near the room, seeming to spend most of his time sat in front of the basement door like a sentinel, guarding it religiously. But rather than scare or creep her out, she found it comical. Maybe that's where the ghost of whoever was apparently haunting this place had died, like a cliché horror movie.

Her thoughts returned to the neighbours' kid, Peter, and whatever had scared him so badly. His parents had glared at her like it was her fault, as if she had purposefully laid a trap to scare him. They had bundled him up and left abruptly, and the way they didn't even say goodbye suggested they wouldn't be returning soon. That was a shame, because she had really wanted to question them about the history of the house. It also meant that if they shunned her, life was going to get pretty lonely around here. She was already missing her friends from Peterborough, and this was not a good way to make new friends. *Maybe I'll pop over later, see how he is and apologise.* But for what she didn't know.

Peter had come bursting into the living room, screaming his head off about a monster in the basement, a little girl covered in blood who wanted to eat him. She was sure he was exaggerating, but the fact he had mentioned a little girl coincided with what she and John had already discussed. But it was a harmless ghost, if she existed at all. She had done nothing to either her or John except scare them a little by being so unexpected. And really, whether ghosts existed or not, which she was still undecided on, ghosts couldn't physically harm people. Not unless they gave you a heart attack, of course, but that wasn't going to happen here. No, Peter had just scared himself shitless by going into the basement in the first place, which was his own fault—she had specifically told him not to go down there in case he tripped and fell.

At least she wouldn't have to worry about kids running around the house. Although it should have been something delightful and pleasurable, hearing a child running about laughing and playing, she still wasn't quite ready for that. It brought back painful memories, a dozen 'what if' questions she didn't want to answer. Not yet, not now. It might have been two years since that day, but it might as well have been yesterday. John still acted uncomfortable whenever they were around kids, not sure what to say for fear of saying something that might hurt her unintentionally, and she loved him for it.

A busy and potentially enjoyable day ahead of her, she dragged herself out of bed, wrapped herself in her robe, and headed downstairs to make coffee. As she had predicted, Sparky sat in front of the basement door expectantly. She reached down to stroke him, yet he completely ignored her.

"What is it with you and that door? Is there a ghostie down there you want to play with?"

She thought of opening the door and seeing what he did, but thoughts of Peter and the hole he said he had seen in the wall came back. John had gone down there but hadn't seen a thing. It didn't mean it wasn't there though—perhaps hidden behind junk—and the last thing she needed was the cat getting in there and lost. But, happy Sparky wasn't running around the place breaking stuff, she left him to it.

After she had finished breakfast, she had a shower then went into the living room to hang up the new curtains she had bought yesterday. She had been tempted to buy curtains for the whole house, but they were still on something of a budget until John got paid at the end of a month, so she refrained from doing so. As she hung the beige curtains, there was a light thud from upstairs, as if something small had fallen over. She ignored it, guessing already it may be her new, mischievous, little friend. There was another, followed by the sound of the cat shrieking. He burst into the living room and hid behind the sofa.

"Don't be such a wimp, cat," she yelled at him, giggling. After shopping, she decided she would open her laptop, too, find out a bit more about this place if possible. Maybe the little girl had died here and was still hanging around. The thought made her sad, not just for the unhappy spirit but for herself. She wondered if there was a minimum age required to become a ghost, then quickly banished the thought from her mind. She didn't want to think about those things.

"I'm off shopping, Sparky. Behave and stop acting like a coward. No one's going to hurt you, you big baby."

The cat ignored her, sulking behind the sofa, so she left to head into town, glad John had rented a car to get to the office until they could buy another.

Even though she had plenty to do, her mind kept coming back to the house's history. She spent most of the morning wandering around the small marketplace and window shopping in the adjacent shops. One shop in particular grabbed her attention. It was a small one that sold all kinds of occult books, gifts, and assorted items. She was tempted to pop in, speak to the owner about their little guest at home, but refrained. She could see the owner through the window, her long, brown hair cascading over her face as she flicked through a book. Another day, perhaps.

By midday she was starting to get hungry, so she made her way home and carried the seeds for the garden into the house. Again, as before, the cat was sitting in his usual spot, having apparently got over his earlier fright.

"Hello again, you! Feeling braver now?"

The cat ignored her. She carried the bags to the kitchen, put everything away, then went to the living room to grab her laptop. Halfway in she stopped. Her new curtains were lying in a heap on the floor.

"What the hell! That's not funny!" she yelled. It had taken her ages to put them up, balancing delicately on the stepladder, and it certainly hadn't been the cat that had ripped them down. Suddenly, the idea of living with a ghost didn't seem quite as romantic as it had before. Especially if it was a bored, mischievous one.

"You leave my curtains alone!" she yelled. "Find something else to do!"

She scooped up the curtains and threw them on the sofa, meaning to put them back later. Her interest was now in the house's past, not present. She grabbed her laptop and fired it up. That seemingly casual glance between the neighbours hadn't gone forgotten. They knew something and weren't telling the whole truth. At least that was the assumption she had made. Carrie had also said the police had been to the house on many occasions, accompanied by forensics officers refusing to divulge any information other than asking if they had seen the neighbours or knew of their whereabouts. That was ominous.

Had they really divorced and all gone their separate ways, or…?

Cathy shuddered at the thought. That wasn't as romantic either. She was about to type in the address of her new home when she heard a noise upstairs. She glanced at the living room door, wide open, to see the cat curled up in front of the basement, so it wasn't him that had knocked something over again. She heard it once more. It wasn't something that had been knocked over, but the faint sound of someone sobbing. A girl. Curious and smiling, she set down her laptop and headed upstairs, passing the cat, which had awoken having obviously heard it, too, and who was snarling in the back of his throat.

As she rose up the stairs, it came again, from her bedroom. Soft wailing as though coming from outside. It made the hair on the back of her neck rise prominently, tingling with static. Not in the slightest scared or concerned, Cathy continued until she was standing outside the bedroom. If it was the ghost supposedly haunting her home, she was obviously upset about something. Had it been her who pulled the curtains down? The snivelling and sobbing continued until Cathy opened the door, when it abruptly ceased.

"Hello? Don't be afraid. Who are you? What do you want?" she asked, feeling a little embarrassed at talking to a potential ghost. But no one answered. Instead, Cathy gasped when she saw the state of the opposite wall. Someone or something had scribbled on the wall. Or scratched onto it more like, marks as though sharp fingernails had cut into the plaster. The word 'FIND' was written in long, scraggly letters.

Chapter 11

Cathy groaned and mumbled in her sleep, restless. In the deep subconscious of her mind, she somehow knew she was dreaming but couldn't in any way control what was happening. She found herself wearing her pyjamas, sprawled on a filthy mattress in the basement. She could barely see a thing down there, the grimy old lightbulb swinging back and forth above her like a pendulum, casting a dark, orange haze around her. Grotesque shadows formed on the walls, growing bigger then diminishing or vanishing completely, that resembled Lovecraftian monsters.

She looked around, wondering why she would have ended up down here let alone fell asleep. She couldn't remember a thing. There was no reason to be down here. It was dusty and smelled of mildew and was surely filled with spiders. Just the thought of that made her quickly jump up and check the mattress, but with the light so dim it was hard to tell. The swinging lightbulb was creating all kinds of small and large things to miraculously appear. Cathy tried to reach up to it, stop it swinging, but it was too high. It was making her dizzy, as though slowly hypnotising her. It occurred to her there was no reason for it to be swinging in the first place. It was quiet and calm down here—no thuds on the ceiling or anything to cause it to happen.

She realised she was cold and picked up the blanket, wrapping it around her. As she glanced around the room, she noticed there was something wrong about the basement; the layout was different to how she remembered it. It wasn't filled with junk and boxes but was in a reasonably clean-looking state and mostly empty, as if it had been recently tidied and was in regular use. The wall where all the junk had been stacked against was gone, and it looked as though it might have been built at a much later date, the bricks still new, not crumbling or covered in old paint.

But this was all irrelevant. What wasn't was getting out of here and back to her proper bed. She was still cold despite the blanket hugged tightly to her body, and there was something about being here that made her extremely uncomfortable and claustrophobic.

The lightbulb continued swinging back and forth, like an angry cat's tail, as she headed towards the door at the top of the stairs. When she reached it and turned the handle, the first sliver of panic crawled up her spine. It wouldn't budge. She grabbed the handle with both hands, pushing as hard as she could, sobs escaping from now very dry lips. When that didn't work, she banged at the door with her fists, screaming for John to wake up and come and get her, but after a few minutes of that and no sign of John coming for her, she gave up and sank to the floor, sobbing hysterically. She was going to die down here, starve to death, unless she survived on whatever bugs and spiders she could catch. Someone had locked her in the basement for whatever reason and thrown away the key.

There was a noise behind her, a shuffling sound or something scratching at the walls. Her body immediately tightened, painfully so, as if her muscles were contracting, squeezing her heart tighter against her ribcage. Cathy really didn't want to turn around and see what it was but couldn't help herself. When she heard the distant sobbing and snivelling, her head shot back around again, facing the wall, her bladder dangerously close to unleashing its contents.

The noise reached a crescendo, so it seemed there wasn't just one person stuck in here with her but several, all coming from the same spot—directly behind her. She tried to tell herself she had been thrust into a nightmare, that soon she would wake up in her own bed and tomorrow she would be laughing about all this with John over coffee and toast. But right now that wasn't helping much. She also told herself that being a nightmare, nothing could really hurt her, so turn around, see whatever it is that's scaring you, and it will go away. But she couldn't bring herself to do it. She sat there like an inmate in some mental institution, huddled on the floor, her knees brought up under her chin, shaking with fear.

"Cathy?" came a weak, pleading voice. "Please help us. We beg you."

"Go away," she whimpered. "Leave me alone. It's not funny anymore."

"Cathy," they sang in unison, a ghostly trio whose melodic voices were anything but heavenly; instead, their voices gurgled as though their throats were filled with some thick liquid. "We need you, Cathy. You have to find him."

She tried to ignore them, hoping they would fade or go away. Yet, there was resistance on her behalf, as if some invisible hand was tugging at her mind and body, forcing her to turn and face them. She resisted, covering her eyes with her hands like a child playing hide and seek while her friend sought to hide, but at the same time she found herself turning regardless.

And instantly regretted it.

Three figures stood at the far corner of the basement, shimmering golden under the grim, orange glow of the lightbulb. One of them was much taller than the other two, who appeared to be children. It was hard to tell; their faces were covered in thick, dark blood, like oil, that dripped slowly to the floor and down their clothes. All three had their hands over their faces, too, as if playing the same game as Cathy, only this time their presence was all too obvious, as were their eyes, white like marbles, peeking out from between splayed fingers.

The three silhouetted figures hovered above the floor, their bare feet dangling inches above it, a constant drip from their toes forming a black, slick pool beneath them. Cathy wanted to scream. Scream herself awake or away from this nightmare, anywhere but here. Surely this couldn't be the mischievous little girl haunting their home.

"Look at us, Cathy. You need to help us. You have to," they sang together, yet it was barely a whisper.

Sobbing, Cathy shook her head but raised it at the same time, her eyes as though someone was prodding them open. The adult and two children held their arms out to her, beckoning her with ghostly fingers, their heads cocked at strange angles as if straining to hear some distant sound. While they were semi-transparent, the wall behind them still visible, she could also make out the terrible gashes on their bodies, the blood flowing freely as though real, the sound of each drop plopping onto the growing pool echoing around the empty room as though it was raining heavily.

"Please, go away," whimpered Cathy again. "Leave me alone. I can't help you."

A grumble resounded around the basement, like a fast-approaching train. The walls shook, the lightbulb swung so hard it nearly hit the ceiling with each swing, monstrous shadows flickered everywhere. Cathy staggered backwards, wanting to get as far away from them as possible yet knowing she was trapped down here, at least until she woke up. If she woke up.

The wall that in real life had had all the junk and boxes piled up against it rumbled, brick dust falling from between the cracks like ash, spouting out as if blown by some volcanic eruption. Then, from between the bricks, a dark, rusty-coloured substance leaked, as though the wall itself was shedding crimson tears. It spilled down the walls as the three ghostly apparitions stared at Cathy, their eyes like distant planets in the night sky. Something wet and sticky pooled around Cathy's feet. When she looked down, she was horrified to see the blood seeping from the wall had almost covered the entire floor already. She backed away, praying she didn't stumble and fall in her horror and panic, soaking up all that gore with her thin pyjamas.

"Help us, Cathy. You have to help us. Find him."

"I can't help you! Find who?" she wailed.

"You know who. Search for him in locked rooms."

"Just…just go away! Leave me alone!"

And then, when she thought her terror couldn't reach any higher level, when madness would leave her a pathetic, drooling mess forever, banging her head against the padded walls of Northgate Hospital for the Mentally Impaired, she heard the soft crying of a baby that seemed to come from behind the bleeding wall. Its wailing reached her broken, pierced heart, shattering what was left of her sanity. She covered her ears, trying to block it out, screaming herself to avoid hearing that baby's wail, even though the sound was coming as much from the exterior of her soul as from within.

Cathy clutched her stomach as though the sound was coming from there, too, and in a way it was, a grim reminder of tragic events both past and present.

"Help us, Cathy. You have no choice. Help us or join us."

In the split second after the spirit finished, it was as though time stopped. The blood stopped running down the walls and disappeared, as did the ghosts. The wailing ceased and the lightbulb stopped swinging manically back and forth, then the basement door slowly creaked open allowing clean light to rid the gloominess from the room. Cathy wasted no time and ran up the stairs, the ghostly baby's wailing still ringing in her ears, until she reached her bedroom and jumped into bed. She slapped a snoring John, trying to rouse him, tell him what she knew and maybe even the dreaded secret that had been burdening her for so long, but no matter how hard she slapped him, he refused to waken. She was still in her nightmare, so she turned over and stared up at the ceiling, sobbing quietly, until she was taken back to another realm and slept peacefully the rest of the night.

Chapter 12

John was smiling as he parked as Peugeot in the car park next to his house. The project he was working on, a series of private homes on a recently developed industrial estate, was moving along better than he imagined. The outlines were made, his boss was pleased, and very soon work would begin on the infrastructure—roads, ADSL cables, sewage and water supplies. It was the biggest job he had ever worked on as lead architect, and his nerves had been frazzled as he planned it all out to the smallest detail. If everything worked out accordingly, his boss had hinted at even bigger jobs, which in turn would mean a bigger bonus. Aside from a new car for both him and Cathy, he was already thinking of turning the basement into a gym and man-cave. Somewhere to bring new friends as he made them, watch football, drink beer while Cathy, hopefully, kept herself amused with new girlfriends. They'd been here nearly a week already, and after what happened with the neighbours' kid the other day, somehow he didn't think the neighbours would be coming over too often. Unless to spy on the haunted house.

He chuckled at the thought of living with ghosts. Cathy especially seemed excited about the prospect, like a kid discovering Santa Claus lived next door. He was happy for her about that; the last couple of years had been particularly tough on her. A part of her had died, too, along with the baby. Perfectly understandable, of course, and he had done to his best to be there for her, giving her time, not smothering her, letting her deal with her grief as she needed while letting her know he was there for her. And now, after two years, the smile was starting to return to her face, the warm, sparkling glow she carried with her like an aura was returning, as was the colour to her face. Maybe, just maybe, it was time to start thinking of trying again.

John grabbed his things, climbed out, and locked it, admiring the tranquillity of his new home and surroundings. No kids racing about screaming and shouting and, more importantly, using the side of his house as a makeshift goal post, no teenagers hanging around corners smoking questionable substances. Where they had lived before moving here had been a haven for drug dealers, and police cars were a constant. He had a feeling they were going to enjoy living here a lot, ghosts or no ghosts. When he had left this morning, Cathy had been fast asleep, which was unusual. Normally the alarm on his phone was enough to stir her from her slumber, but not today. Maybe she had been dreaming about their ghostly friend tearing down the curtains all night.

He was about to open the garden gate when he saw movement in the upstairs bedroom window. Someone was standing there waving to him, silhouetted by the streetlamp beside him. He waved back at Cathy, wondering what she had been up to all day. She had been badgering him about cleaning the basement, finding out whatever it was that interested the cat so much, but that would have to wait until the weekend. He may work sitting down all day, but the mental stress was just as equal as having a physical job. Hungry, John hurried inside and called up to his wife, a little disappointed he couldn't smell anything from the kitchen.

"Hey, honey. What are you doing up there? Hanging more curtains again?"

"Come and see!"

He groaned, hoping the bedroom wall hadn't been scribbled all over again. Romantic or not, if this supposed ghost Cathy insisted on seeing was going to ruin their furniture and walls every day, he told her he would be finding the nearest exorcist he could and banishing the thing off to Heaven or wherever they went. There was no way he was spending his bonus on refurbishing every other day. John headed upstairs, slightly concerned at what he was about to be shown, yet when he entered his bedroom, he stopped abruptly. The room was empty.

There were no crude scribbles on the walls, no new curtains proudly dangling above the window, but more importantly, no sign of Cathy, either.

"Cathy? Where are you?"

"I'm in here!"

He left and headed in the direction of her voice to the spare bedroom. He went in and stopped again, looking everywhere, including behind the door, in case this was some kind of a game.

"Cathy, c'mon, I'm hungry. Where are you hiding?"

"I'm in here!" came again, but now from the bedroom he had just left. Now his smile wasn't as prominent. It sure as hell sounded like Cathy, but unless she had been hiding under the bed or in the wardrobe, which he doubted…

This time he didn't reply, instead returning as quietly as possible to catch Cathy or whoever was imitating her off guard. He crept towards the bedroom door and burst in. It was empty.

"Okay, you've had your fun," he said, feeling foolish. "Ha ha!" John left the room and made to go downstairs, phone Cathy to see where she was, when he halted.

A young boy and girl were standing at the bottom of the stairs, looking up at him solemnly, dressed in tattered pyjamas, holes cut into the filthy fabric.

"Hello?" John muttered, his lips suddenly very dry. "What are you doing in my house? You live around here? You shouldn't trespass you know; it's against the law."

They said nothing but continued looking at him, a smile now forming on their lips. John was lost for words, a shiver of unease rippling through him. He wondered if it had been these kids calling to him from upstairs; but if so, how had they managed to get downstairs again without him seeing? And if they were…no, that was impossible—they were as solid and real as he was.

"I asked you a question. What are you doing in my home? Where do you live? I'm going to speak to your parents."

Still they said nothing, staring at him with creepy grins on their faces. He felt like a prisoner in his own home, wanting to go down the stairs and drag them to their parents but afraid to get any closer to them, as though they were dangerous and might harm him. The fact they said nothing, standing there, their arms dangling by their sides, looking malnourished, made him wonder. Cathy had said she had heard a young girl giggling and sobbing on occasions. Is that what he was looking at now—a bona fide *ghost*?

"What's the matter? Can't you speak? I'm going to phone the police if you don't go." He felt stupid for being scared and threatened by a couple of kids, but his body was screaming at him something was very wrong here. It was one thing pretending their home might be haunted to keep Cathy amused; it was another to have two of them at the bottom of his stairs making the hairs on his body prickle with unease. Deciding he couldn't stay here all night and wondering just where the fuck Cathy was right now to bail him out of this situation, he took a tentative step down the stairs, expecting the two kids to run off. But they remained passive and motionless just as before, grinning inane grins. He was sure, for the briefest of moments, that he could see the wall through them.

"I-I'm not gonna tell you again. Get the fu—"

There was movement below him. A shadow. At first, he thought it was the basement door swinging open again, just as Cathy had mentioned, but the shadow glided along the hallway until it stopped at the two creepy kids.

"What are you doing here, scaring the poor man? C'mon, get out. It's not him you want to see anyway."

The owner of the voice looked up at John. It was a woman, presumably their mother, but there was something about her he didn't like either. Her skin was too pallid, her milky eyes as though she had cataracts, almost completely white and with no discernible pupils. John wanted to scream. He thought he might be about to do so, too, when she smiled at him, her mouth opening slightly to show rotting gums, but then she turned and left, the two children following after her.

John stood there shocked, dumbfounded, not knowing what to say or think. Was he imagining this? Were they real? Who were they and how did the mother know the kids were here? What if they weren't real? What did that mean? He took another step then realised his legs were extremely weak. He had to grab onto the railing; he noticed his hands were shaking. He had been holding his breath for far too long. It occurred to him that if Cathy wasn't here, the front and back doors would be locked—he had unlocked the front door himself—so how had they got in and why didn't he hear the back door close after the three left? If they had broken in, something would need fixing.

Despite not really wanting to but knowing he couldn't stand here all night, he forced himself down the stairs, half expecting the three creepy people to be standing in his kitchen still. But as he looked along the hallway to the kitchen, there was no one there. And the back door was closed. A part of him considered phoning the police right now, tell them they had had intruders. But if just a few days after moving in police cars started appearing at their home, lights flashing, it wasn't going to make their job of making new friends around here any easier. Besides, he still wasn't convinced what he had just witnessed had been exactly what his brain was trying to tell him. When he reached the kitchen, tried the back door and found it locked, a cold chill seized his heart, paralysing his muscles.

He stood with his hand on the door for several seconds, trying to process everything, when it occurred to him they might still be in the house. He rushed around the dining room and living room, checking behind the doors even, then the basement door, which was locked, and forced himself to stop. They weren't here. There was no way they could have gone out the front door, and the windows were all closed, but why would they climb out the window anyway? For the first time, the possibility Cathy may indeed have been right formed in his mind, and he didn't like it. Not at all.

"Fuck this, I need a drink," he muttered and headed to the drink cabinet. He poured himself a healthy shot of whiskey and knocked it back, his head reeling, his intestines squirming. He hadn't been so freaked out in his life. Once, as a kid, he and some friends had gone to a graveyard in the middle of the night with a makeshift Ouija board. Sat on the wet grass, beers in their hands, they had tried to summon one of the deceased and failed spectacularly, until they had heard a rustling behind a nearby tree and what might have been growling. Convinced they had just summoned the most evil of demons, they had bolted, only for one of them to turn back and see a dog sniffing around the area. At first that had scared the hell out of him, but that was nothing compared to this. Not in some grimy old graveyard, but here in his new home, where he lived and slept with his wife. What if they came back when he was asleep, opening his eyes to see them standing over him?

He poured another shot then moved back to the kitchen, deciding to open the back door and check if there were footprints, but just as he was about to unlock the back door, he happened to glance at the fridge-freezer. Cathy had bought some magnets in the shape of letters yesterday, among other things, to decorate the fridge with, spelling out John's name and a rather crude word next to it, but now it was gone. Instead, there was another word placed there roughly, as though a child had done it.

KARL.

And next to that, just beneath it, the letters A, F, O, I, N, and D.

He stared at it. Karl? Who was Karl? Karla? Cathy's mother was Karla. Maybe she had been playing about absently. He ignored it and had returned to the back door, when the front door opened and Cathy walked in. She smiled when she saw him, carrying some shopping bags, but her smile wavered when she entered the kitchen.

"John? What's wrong? You're as pale as a ghost. Seen our friendly little ghost, have you?"

John didn't find that funny. Her told her what had happened, and the expression on her face suggested either she didn't believe him or he was making it up.

"I'm not joking, Cathy. There were two kids standing there, then their mother came in and took them away. And the back door is locked. I was just about to go outside and check for footprints, because if they were real, I wanna know why and how the hell they got in my house."

That wiped the smirk from Cathy's face as she contemplated the insinuations. "We'll knock on all the neighbour's doors tomorrow, see if you recognize them."

"Then they'll think we're weird. Oh, and did you rearrange the magnets?"

He pointed to the fridge, and it was Cathy's turn to gasp as the blood drained from her face.

Chapter 13

"Are you okay, Susanne? You look tired and jaded," asked Jeanne, a regular to her little shop.

Susanne offered a weak smile. No, she wasn't alright. Yes, she was tired and jaded. Scared might be another adjective to add on. She had barely been able to sleep at night after what happened with Dennis and Agatha the other day. That voice in her head, the threats to both her and Sally, then the total destruction of their property, had been enough to convince Susanne what her subconscious had already told her the last time—stay away.

"I'm okay," she lied. "Just been rather busy lately with readings and such. I guess I need a holiday, but the shop won't run by itself!"

"I know. You work so hard, it's a shame. But don't work so hard you make yourself ill."

Jeanne paid for her items and left, leaving Susanne to stare at her as she went.

'Make yourself ill.' That was exactly what she was doing to herself. Scaring herself to death, and for good reason. Several times she had thought of phoning Agatha to see if they were okay, but the way she had screamed at her to get out, the look of utter terror in her eyes, Susanne was pretty sure the woman would just scream abuse at her and tell her never to phone or go near her again. Which, to an extent, she could understand. It was clear Agatha's apparent sincerity about treating Vera as best they could was a lie—Dennis had said as much—so surely she had to accept part of the blame lay with her. If they hadn't mistreated Vera so badly, warranted or not, Vera wouldn't have carried so much anger with her. All Susanne had done was what she had been asked. But the severity with which Vera had destroyed their home, the demon threatening her to keep away or harm both her and her daughter, she could never in a million years have expected such ferocity.

She had to give it up, just as she had told herself the last time. Sally would understand, and so would the Soul Searchers, although she would miss them terribly. They had become a second family to her over the years, but now she could be putting their souls at risk, if she hadn't already; for all she knew, the demon had already claimed them. So no, it was no surprise she probably looked quite pallid and ill. She felt ill, ready to vomit at any second, barely able to come to the shop in the mornings and open up, but if she didn't, she could forget all about that little cottage. She could forget about everything.

She thought about closing and leaving for lunch seeing as it was midday, but she wasn't hungry either. It was another thing she had lost—her appetite—but she knew if she didn't get something inside her…well, as she told Jeanne, if she didn't open up in the mornings, no one would. Across the road was a café that made fresh sandwiches she had often went to so figured a toasted cheese sandwich should stay in her stomach long enough. She was about to leave when the phone rang.

"Hello?"

"Hi, is that Susanne? Susanne Hill?"

"Yes, it is. Who am I speaking to?"

"Hi. Umm, I'm Jill. A friend gave me your number. It's…I mean, I don't really believe in this stuff, at least I didn't until recently. But, well, a friend died recently, and I think I've started seeing their spirit or something in my home. I can smell their perfume nearby when I'm alone, things move from their spot or in different places than where I left them. I hear my name being whispered, and I'm pretty sure it's my friend calling to me. I was wondering if it was possible to contact her, see what she wants? I don't have a lot of money, but I could pay you, and I'm getting pretty desperate by now. It's starting to intensify. I hear her screaming sometimes, like from a long way away. I really want to know what she wants. Please?"

Susanne groaned. "I'm sorry, but I don't do that anymore. You'll have to find someone else. I'm sorry."

"But…my friend highly recommended you. She said you helped her enormously, and I don't trust anyone else. Please. I'll pay you."

"It's not about the money, and I did it for free anyway. But…I had a bad experience recently and I vowed never to do it again. You'll have to find someone else. Sorry."

She made to hang up, feeling terrible for denying this person the opportunity to connect with their friend, but a promise was a promise.

"But wait! Don't hang up. I'm really desperate, and there isn't anyone else I can trust. You have to help me, just this once."

"I'm sorry, but no. Not anymore."

She hung up and took a deep breath. Tears welled in her eyes as a sense of betrayal overcame her. Susanne had been very tempted to say 'Yes, okay, one last time,' and had to force herself not to. There could be no going back to that world, not unless she wanted to forfeit her life and soul. The phone rang again. She considered not answering, but unless she was firm with this woman, she could harass her for days.

"I'm sorry, but you need to stop harassing me or I'll report this number to the police. Please, I'm not willing to take on any more work again."

"Susanne? Susanne Hill?"

She winced. It was a man's voice, not the previous caller.

"Umm, yes. Sorry, I thought you were someone else. How may I help you?"

There was a long silence, and for a moment she thought he had hung up although she could still hear his shallow breathing.

"Hello?"

"I…I want you to know. What you did. I told her it was a mistake, that she should have just tried to ignore it, but she wouldn't listen. She never listened. We both knew the real reasons this was happening, and nothing short of an exorcist was going to stop her. Miserable old bitch was a witch even when she died."

"I'm sorry, who is this? I have no idea what you're talking about."

"No? You don't know? I thought you were a psychic. One of them mediums who could see the future."

"No, I'm not. I've never been able to see the future, but you haven't answered my question."

"You killed her. Despite everything, you still brought this on. If you'd let well enough alone, this might not have happened, and my wife…"

She thought she heard sobbing coming from the other end. An inkling of who was calling formed in her mind, and she really wanted to hang up, but curiosity got the better of her.

"…my wife would still be alive."

"I'm sorry. I think you have the wrong person. I don't know what you're talking ab—"

"Agatha, you fool! She's dead, she killed herself!"

Susanne froze midway towards hanging up the phone. Her mind reeled with the news and the possibilities. The immediate thought that bombarded her devastated brain was the demon had kept true to its word. It had broken through and killed Agatha, maybe using her mother as an anchor. And now it was going to come for her. After somehow bringing Sally back from her resting place.

"But…but how? It's impossible."

"Impossible? How can you say that? You saw what happened in my home. Was that impossible too? You did that. You pushed my wife over the edge."

"Mr…(*shit, what's his surname?*) Dennis. I swear it wasn't me. It was your mother-in-law. You heard what she said. You told me yourself that your wife had been mistreating her. All I did was communicate with her and relay her message. I had no idea that was going to happen. Did you see it happen? Did you see the entity kill your wife?"

"Entity? What the hell are you talking about, you mad woman? She killed herself! Took an overdose then slit her wrists during the night. She was already dead when I woke up in the middle of the night. And I want you to know you caused this. If you'd stayed away, we could have learned to live with it. I should call the police."

Susanne didn't know what to say. Part of her felt an enormous relief the demon hadn't broken through the invisible barrier between the afterlife and Earth, but that this poor woman had decided to end her own life through guilt was terribly tragic as well. And yet, another part of her, a side to her she barely remembered, was feeling rage. Anger at this man who dared accuse of her of driving his wife to suicide when it had been both of them who had begged for her help. If anyone was guilty it was the pair of them for practically starving the old woman and leaving her to fester in her own filth.

"I'm very sorry for your loss, but how dare you accuse me of causing your wife's death. You both insisted that I come to your home and try and make contact, which I did. And then you decided to tell me that you hadn't been treating your mother-in-law with exactly the best care and attention, so no, I'm sorry, but this is not on me. Had I known your mother-in-law was so angry with the pair of you, I would probably have refused to even try. Contacting an angry spirit is a very dangerous thing, as you saw for yourself. So if you want to phone the police go ahead, but this has nothing to do with me."

"Bullshit! You fucking killed my wife and you're gonna pay for it, one way or the other. You can expect a visit from me at some point."

"Is that a *threat*? Are you *threatening* me? How dare you?"

Soul Searchers

She waited for a response, her fingers hurting from holding the phone so tightly to her ear, but Dennis had already hung up. She slammed her phone on the table, wanting to burst out crying at the sheer audacity of the man. Yet at the same time, she desired to rush to *his* house and tell him to his face it was their own damn fault. It also meant she would have to keep one eye on her surroundings in case he decided to carry out his threat. Susanne might be a frail-looking woman, but appearances could be deceiving. She had taken her fair share of self-defence classes when she was younger, and nothing or nobody was going to put her life in danger and make her act paranoid. *Let him come and get me*, she told herself. *I'll be waiting.*

Chapter 14

Hot water cascaded over Cathy as she rubbed shower gel over her body. The water was as hot as she could stand without burning herself, and even then her body was red like she had been in the sun for too long. She wanted the heat to reach her insides, burn out the parasite gnawing away at her intestines making her feel nauseous. Suddenly, her new house had changed rapidly and dramatically from being warm and cheerful with the added romantic bonus of having a little girl's spirit keeping her company to ominous and cold. A place that instead of filling her with joy and excitement about upcoming projects, ideas on how to paint and decorate it further, now made her feel a certain dread every time she was left alone, jumping at the slightest sound or movement, scared to turn around for fear of what she might see or find. Earlier, the cat had ran past her, playing, and she almost screamed, her heart leaping up into her throat, thinking it was something else.

When she had come home last night and John had told her about what he saw, she had assumed he was joking, trying to scare her. Once, a few years ago on Halloween, he had hidden in the wardrobe, waiting for her to come upstairs, and had jumped out at her wearing a Michael Myers mask. He had found it utterly hilarious; Cathy nearly died of fright. The other night he had told her not to let her toes stick out from beneath the blanket, and not just because Sparky might see them as a wonderful new toy to bite but in case a cold, clammy hand grabbed her ankle and tried to drag her out of bed. She had laughed and told him he should be worried about the same thing—except it might not be his toes their ghost grabbed ahold of with clammy hands but something far more delicate.

She didn't really know if the house was haunted or not, it just seemed a fun concept to entertain, something to amuse herself with when here all alone. Ghosts weren't scary, that was just for the movies. All the books she had ever read spoke of some harmless presence, perhaps the odd thing moved from its original spot, a spirit that hadn't completely accepted its life was over and wanted to remain. She thought that might have been the case with the ghostly little girl keeping them company, but that all changed when John told his story.

Because she had seen that exact cast of characters in her nightmare. That wasn't a coincidence. She hadn't told him about the three figures in the basement begging her for help, hadn't told him that when she had ignored them, the blood had run down the wall like the water running down her now. About how they had threatened her—*you have no choice*—and the sound of a baby wailing. She knew what that wailing represented, who the owner of it was, but even then she had put it all down to a particularly bad and realistic nightmare.

Until now.

And yet, she could still pass it off as some bizarre coincidence, the spirits in the house playing with them, having a little fun at their expense. But when she had seen the way the magnets had been rearranged on the fridge, all thoughts of a coincidence and playful spirits dissolved as fast as her dreams of this being innocent and romantic.

She knew that name. Karl. It hadn't been the name of her mother; perhaps whatever spirit had changed the letters about had added that extra A as a warning. *We know. Everything. Help us or we'll reveal all.* And Cathy would die before telling John the truth.

She could tell from John's expression, his eyes squinting as though lost in thought, that the jumbled letters had far more significance than she was letting on. Seeing that had scared Cathy a thousand times more than John's account of ghostly children at the foot of the stairs, and the loud gasp she had produced upon seeing the fridge probably alerted him to the fact.

It changed everything. It meant that these spirits—now apparently not a little girl but two children and possibly their mother—very badly wanted something from them and were evidently prepared to do whatever it took to get her to listen. But what? She thought about what the neighbours had said. The whole family before them had suddenly disappeared, father and husband included, so that seemed a pretty good start. Had the father killed his kids and wife and then himself? It was a possibility, but how was she going to prove it if they hadn't been seen since? One of them had scribbled the word 'FIND' on the bedroom wall, so that was a good indicator she was heading in the right direction, as were the instructions the ghost had given her in her dream, '*Find him.*' That had to be the answer then. The owner of this house had killed his family, then himself, and they wanted him found. But if he was already dead, what was she supposed to do—dig him up and piss on his grave or something? Throw his bones in the sewer? Where was she even going to start looking? Her, a new girl on the block who barely knew the way to the town centre.

She guessed the best place to start would be what she had intended doing the other day—search on the internet for any newspaper or blog reports of the sudden disappearance. Surely there had to be something somewhere: an enterprising neighbour, a kid, perhaps, who had been intrigued by the events and had kept some kind of electronic journal, his mind wild with all kinds of conspiracy theories. She imagined Facebook accounts set up to chronicle ghostly sightings in the windows; kids daring to break in and wander around the house, recording their movements; theories on where the bodies might be buried.

Now that she had something to at least work towards, Cathy turned off the shower and stepped out. She was going to have to work fast, solve this riddle before the spirits became restless again. All she could do was pray they were watching over her, knew she was at least trying to help them so they would refrain from leaving more cryptic messages. As she dried herself off, the bathroom was like being stuck in a thick fog with how long she had stood under the near boiling water. But as the steam dissipated and she finished drying her hair with a towel, she took a step backwards, almost tripping over her wet feet. Written onto the steamy mirror in crude, childish letters was the word KARL. In that instant, wailing echoed around the house, a baby's cry for help.

Cathy crashed against the wall in her shock, staring at that word, shaking her head. Her body which only moments before had been scalding hot was now covered in goosebumps, her skin icy. She shivered, tears replacing the hot water that had soaked her face. The wailing was so desperate it was like a baby starving to death somewhere. It resounded around the house, in her head, incessant and haunting.

"Please, stop!" she cried. "I'll find him! I'll do what you asked, but please just stop!"

It did. Suddenly, the only sounds were her heavy breathing and sniffing, the accusatory word on the mirror fading to nothing. It occurred to her then she really did have no choice but to comply with their demands. It was that or move out of the house they had only paid one mortgage payment on. And what exactly was she supposed to tell John? That the ghosts had discovered her secret and they needed to get out of here now before he found out as well? That could never happen. *Maybe I could fake an injury. Throw myself down the stairs or something. That would make him believe me if I said the ghosts weren't friendly after all. He was shit scared himself last night. He'd have to believe me.*

But where would they go? Back to Peterborough, start all over again? And where would they get the money to buy another place without selling this one first? The answer was obvious—they weren't.

It wasn't even the fact they were living with a family of ghosts that scared them on occasions. It was the simple yet brutal fact they knew about the abortion. But how? No one in the world knew except her. Right?

###

It should never had happened in the first place. She was pretty sure she'd taken all the necessary precautions, but after a few days of nausea and having missed her period, she didn't need to be a gynaecologist to appreciate the symptoms. And the test she bought from the pharmacy proved her right. She was pregnant.

It was a disaster. The worst kind imaginable. She wasn't even thirty yet and had only been with John a short while. What was he going to say if she told him? He was just starting out his new career, a very promising one that would be hindered if he knew about the baby. But that, of course, was completely irrelevant because John wouldn't be hanging around to see it born. He would leave her to pursue his architectural career, which was what mattered to him more than anything right now. Besides Cathy, obviously.

After staring at that stupid little thing wishing it would magically change to negative instead of positive, she burst into tears. Her world was crumbling before her. If she had been a teenager and drunk at some party she could understand, no matter how much of an idiot she called herself, but she was nearly thirty, studying to be a nurse, while things were steadily becoming more serious with John. She had already vowed to happily give up her career later in life to father John's child, but not now. Five or ten years down the road she would be more than happy to bring up their child while he fulfilled his dream of setting up his own company. Now, all that was over and more.

She had already confided to her best friend, Suzy, that the chances were high, and now the two of them sat together, arms wrapped tightly around each other as Suzy listened to her hysterics.

"What are you going to do?" she asked.

"What can I do? If I tell John, he'll leave me. I can't very well pretend it will go away, can I? Why did I have to be so stupid? My parents will kill me. I love John a lot, but nothing I say is going to change his mind. How could it? I've betrayed him."

"There are other options, you know," said Suzy gently.

Cathy looked up at her friend and wiped her eyes. Surely, she wasn't suggesting…? "But that's murder, Suzy. I couldn't do that. It's a living human being. I'm not religious or anything, but I still think having an abortion is tantamount to murder. Even though it isn't even formed yet. I can't!"

"I get that, Cathy, but you don't have many other choices, do you? Have the baby and lose John or lose the baby and have John. Unless…"

She let the third possibility hang in the air, and there was no need for her to finish it. That was definitely not going to happen. she would bring up the baby on her own if it came to that.

"No. Forget that."

"Okay, well look. You don't have to make a decision right now. Sleep on it, think about it, but I'll tell you now, as your friend, I would have an abortion. We'll keep it a secret between us. No one will ever have to know."

###

No one will ever know.

And until now, that was how it had remained—a closely-guarded secret not even Cathy's parents had suspected. She had spent the week barely able to sleep, lying in bed trying to convince herself what was inside her was not a foetus. She was nauseous because she had eaten something rotten. What was inside her was a simple cell, nothing, insignificant. All she would have to do was go the clinic and pretend she was at the doctors or the dentist—minor check-up, nothing else. And so, after a week of tears, sleepless nights, and John asking her what the hell was wrong with her, she could take it no longer. She went to the nearest clinic and told them to get rid of it. She had cried a week after that, too, telling John about the supposed miscarriage and she needed some time alone.

Poor John was clueless to this day, but that soon might change because no, it wasn't Cathy and Suzy's big secret anymore. Unless Suzy had somehow developed the ability to converse with ghosts as well, the ones living here also knew. That and more.

And it was time to do something about it, or there was a very good chance she might lose John again. John and everything else.

Chapter 15

"Maybe we talked it up. I dunno, like by both talking about it being haunted so much we actually invented the ghosts. Like mass hysteria, our collective minds working overtime and creating something that isn't there. But I know what I saw, dammit! That was no hallucination, and it wasn't me who moved those magnets around on the fridge. I'm pretty sure it wasn't your cat either."

John shook his head, unable to remove those images from his mind as he lay in bed with Cathy. He had been thinking about it all day at work, had been very tempted to ask some of his colleagues for their opinions on ghosts and the supernatural, but he was new here still and didn't want any question marks to be raised about his performance. Telling the others what happened to him last night then asking them whether it could be true might mean a lengthy spell at Northgate Hospital. His boss would probably ask him to leave the next day. Unsurprisingly, John had hardly done a damn thing at work today.

"It's not, John. Something happened in this house, and we need to find out what they want. I had that nightmare remember—the two ghostly kids and presumably their mother. Exactly as you described them to me. So unless you can see my dreams at night, I doubt it."

She was right. He was looking to explain an impossible situation into something more mundane and feasible. Which, he thought, was pretty damn logical. He could grasp t the idea of an afterlife if pressed, but vengeful spirits with a cause hanging around the house? Cathy had told him what the neighbours said about the previous owners, and from what she said, it did indeed sound extremely suspicious. People didn't just disappear like that for no reason. Not the entire family, from one day to the next, without leaving a forwarding address so mail could be sent to them. And the police popping by sporadically? Sounded like they were just as concerned. So, if it had been the wife and her two kids he had seen, it stood to reason the father may indeed have killed them then himself. But as Cathy had argued, if he was dead, what were they supposed to be looking for? Find whom, according to that word scribbled on his wall?

"Look, I don't know anything about ghosts or the supernatural, but I'm pretty sure ghosts can't actually hurt people, so I don't think we're in any real danger. They just want us to find someone. As you said, maybe the father's body. Maybe their own, which sounds more likely. Maybe he killed them and buried them somewhere, and they want us to find their bodies and give them a peaceful burial."

"So where do we start? We don't even know how long ago they disappeared. I forgot to ask, although it won't be hard to find out. I could call the estate agent, or we could Google for any information."

Good point. John climbed out of bed and grabbed his laptop sitting on the chest of drawers. He got back in bed, and Cathy cuddled up to him. First he typed in their address, but all he got was a Google maps photo of their street and websites to a few shops and businesses along the road. But as he scrolled down, he came across a blog piece. He clicked on it to see a photo of his house and a damning headline: *What Happened To The Hamshore Family?*

"Here we go," muttered John.

They read the article. It said that on Wednesday, 24 June, the Hamshore family, Matilda and Alex with their children Darren and Jane, were discovered missing from their home after a family friend found the front door open and entered to investigate. All their belongings were there, but more importantly, the upstairs bedroom had been covered in blood as though a massacre had taken place. According to the witness, the walls were still dripping in blood and there were three large pools on the floor beside the bed. The police were called, but to this day, three months later, there were still no bodies or suspects. It was as if all their bodies had vanished into thin air.

Cathy clasped a hand to her mouth. John squirmed nervously.

"Oh my God, John. They were murdered. Here in our bedroom. Right here where we sleep." She jumped out of bed and pressed herself against the wall as though something hideous had just attacked her. Instinctively, John scanned the walls and floor as if he might suddenly stumble upon dried blood stains, his eyes magically working like Luminol.

"It happened nearly two years ago, Cathy. The house has since been repainted and everything. It's not like it happened yesterday."

"But that's not the point! Don't you get it? They were *murdered* in this house! Right here. That's why their spirits are still here; they want us to find their killer. What if we don't? What are they going to do to us? If the police haven't found the bodies or the killer, what chance do we have?"

She looked like she was about to burst into tears or throw up on the new carpet, where not too long ago a large pool of blood had been. He had to admit, as soon as he had read the article a chill had flown up his spine, his body suddenly cold as though a wintery breeze had blown through the house. The fact the previous owners had died horribly in here wasn't something that bothered him especially; what did were the implications. Cathy would probably demand they move immediately, never to set foot in here again, which wasn't going to happen. But there was now a more sinister motive for the ghosts haunting the place. As Cathy had said, where were they supposed to start? And more importantly, he suddenly realised, who had killed the family? If it had been the man of the house, where was he or his body?

"I don't want to be here anymore," blurted out Cathy.

"Cathy, listen, I—"

"No! Two children were killed here, John. We've been seeing their spirits. It's despicable, horrific, and fucking creepy. I want to go to a hotel then move. I'll go back to Peterborough, I don't care, but I can't stay here not knowing what happened."

"Cathy, listen," he said more sternly. "On a practical level, we simply cannot afford to move. We'd have to sell this place first, and that could take months. It's been empty nearly two years before we bought it. Second, you said you wanted to help these ghosts. Especially the two children and especially now that we know they were murdered. You said yourself they can't hurt us; maybe they'll leave us another clue or something. Maybe we could speak to one of those medium people, if they actually exist outside of movies. Or a priest, I dunno, because as I said, we don't have the money to move. I just started a new job, remember? Until I get paid, we're running on fumes.

"And besides, maybe it has nothing to do with them being murdered. If it was the father, why was he never caught? If he committed suicide, where's his body? It doesn't make any sense."

"It makes a lot of sense, John. Find him. That's what the spirits said. Him meaning their father or the killer. Maybe they're buried in this house somewhere. The basement. That's why the fucking cat is so obsessed with the place and refuses to go down there. What if they're buried under the floor?"

"Cathy, the police would have checked the whole house. That would have been their first hypothesis; the father kills his family, buries the bodies, then flees. But they would have caught him by now. His face would be all over the newspapers. The neighbours...The fucking neighbours. They knew the family had been killed in here and didn't tell us. They lied on purpose, the arseholes. Speak to them again. No wonder they ran from here so quickly when their kid got spooked."

He stared at Cathy, analysing her expressions. The haunted, terrified look was slowly fading as she contemplated the possibilities. She knew, deep down, that moving was financially unviable. If she could convince herself to help the spirits find whatever they required to move on, it would give her a sense of purpose. Might even help her come to terms with the miscarriage she suffered—lost one child but helped two more.

While he studied her face, there was a rumble as though a train was passing right outside the window. Sitting up in bed, he could feel the wall tremble, the bed shaking slightly. The lightbulb above his head shook from side to side. There were three loud bangs on the bedroom door, and it flew open. As if in contrast, the bedroom window slammed shut. Distant wailing came from somewhere in the house. Cathy jumped back into bed and huddled up tight to him.

"What is that?" he asked.

"It's *them*! Warning us."

There was a thud on the stairs, followed by another as if something huge was heading up towards them. The wailing became louder, as though its owner was now in the room with them.

"Help!" came a long, drawn out cry.

The door swung on its hinges, imitating the lightbulb. Outside on the landing, a shadow grew just to the left of the open door, soon becoming three elongated forms that flickered and changed shape like dark clouds. The sound of the baby was now under their bed it seemed, yet John refused to check. His body would refuse to answer his frazzled brain's commands anyway. He looked to Cathy, clutching him tightly, her face a mask of terror. He took her hands in his and squeezed. Both their legs were now drawn up to their chests, as though trying to make themselves smaller, invisible to the ghostly entities. A lump lay at the foot of the bed, under the blanket. On another occasion it might have been the cat; he liked to hide under the blankets when it was cold. But cats didn't wail like newborn babies. The thing's chest rose and fell slightly as if breathing, all the time that haunting, chilling wail resonated in their heads.

"Okay! Okay! I said we'll help!" screamed Cathy. "Just tell us what to look for?"

"Him!" came a deep, booming voice that made the walls and their bed shake. Then everything was utterly still and silent.

For several seconds neither said a word, the only movement their chests rising and falling as they gasped for air. They stared into each other's eyes. John was pretty sure his were as wide as Cathy's were, brimming with shocked tears. Then Cathy grabbed and hugged him.

"I guess that answers your questions," he said. "You've got a job to do—find their father."

Chapter 16

The cat had stopped sitting by the basement door, as though he had got bored with his feline fantasises. A dozen mice to chase perhaps, or flapping fish just waiting for him to sink his teeth into for a luxurious meal. Instead, he now spent most of his time in Cathy's bedroom, where previously he had refused to enter. Now that she knew what had taken place there, it freaked her out and caused goosebumps to rise on her arms as the cat sat staring incessantly at the wardrobe. A couple of times she had opened it for him to see what would happen, but the only thing he did was meow and raise his fur, as if in there lurked something completely the opposite of what he suspected lay behind the basement door.

She couldn't take her eyes off the floor and walls, wondering where exactly the pools of blood had been, where their bodies had been slain and with what. It was morbid and she hated herself for it, but sitting there on the bed beside the cat, she couldn't think of anything else. She had considered moving into the spare bedroom, but she didn't want to be alone at night either. She didn't want to be in this house, period, but John was right; they didn't have the money to move, and something tugged at her heart, telling her she had to help these spirits, if only for the children's sakes. As an almost-mother, the pangs of guilt still throbbed in her chest.

It was time to take action, do whatever she could to find answers or risk all her secrets being revealed. They were blackmailing her, but she couldn't find any hate inside her to blame them—it was all her own fault, anyway. The first stop would be in town, gathering a bit more information on what she was dealing with in the first place and to what lengths these spirits might go to ensure she carried out her promise. What they were *capable* of doing. As she and John had discussed, it was only in the movies where they physically harmed people. And that wasn't what concerned her the most. Her marriage may be in jeopardy if she didn't solve the grisly riddle in time.

She left the cat half asleep on the bed as always lately, food in his bowl, and headed off into town. It wasn't the biggest town centre by a long stretch, but she already knew where she wanted to go—the shop she had seen the other day with the fancy, quaint figurines and exotic books with titles such as *The Afterlife Explained, Contacting*

Spirits, and *Dealing with the Dead,* which she had thought sounded a little more gruesome, but in her case, that was exactly what she was dealing with.

She found the shop down a narrow alleyway named Row's End, dating back to the 19 century where it was almost possible for neighbours to lean out their windows and shake hands with those opposite. The shop, *Heavenly Treasures,* was small, but just by looking through the window it seemed amazing how the owner had managed to accumulate so many items in there, the shelves on both sides with barely a space left for new stock. Feeling slightly nervous, not quite sure what to say or ask for, she stepped in, a bell above her head tinkling to announce her presence. It wouldn't have mattered because the same young woman stood behind the counter, her long, brown hair cascading over her face like a curtain as she studied a book laid out before her. When she looked up, Cathy caught the slightest flicker of unease on her face, as if expecting the landlord for not paying last month's rent. Seeing it was a potential customer, she smiled and stood up straight.

"Hi there! Can I help you with anything?"

Cathy hated it when shop owners did that. She liked to browse at her leisure before being assaulted with questions, but given the type of things the shop sold, she figured it was more than legitimate. But now that she had asked, she still wasn't sure what to say.

"Umm, I'm not quite sure. Very nice shop you have! So many different things you have in stock. I guess the afterlife and ghosts and things are a popular subject!"

The smile on the woman's face didn't quite reach her eyes, which bore the beginnings of bags underneath them, betraying what Cathy took to be her age. She looked to be around Cathy's age but seemed to have had a slightly harder life. She wore little to no makeup, which made the wrinkles around the corners of her lips and eyes stand out stronger. But then, Cathy assumed that anyone who ran a shop like this must have reason to be surrounded by paraphernalia related to the afterlife.

"Yes, I suppose it is. One of the few givens in life, of course—death and what comes after it."

"And what do you believe comes after it?"

"Oh, umm, I think it depends on the individual. The kind of life they had here. I have several good books on the subject that deal with that from a variety of perspectives. But all in a…positive way, I should add!"

"So you definitely believe in the afterlife? Silly question, I guess, given the nature of what you sell."

"Yes, I do, but as I said, exactly where one's soul goes to after death…well, it could be for many reasons. Some spirits want to stay behind, they miss loved ones and don't want to leave them; others are happy to move straight on to the next."

"And the ones that don't want to leave because there is something needs doing? Something they perhaps feel needs finishing before they can go? An injustice, perhaps?"

There it was again. That flicker of uncertainty in the woman's eyes. She looked briefly away from Cathy, absently running a hand over a table filled with assorted items such as tarot cards, incense holders, and porcelain figures, as though checking for dust.

"Like I said, it all depends."

Clearly Cathy had touched a nerve here, and she silently cursed herself for being so abrupt and direct. This was not the way to get answers to the questions she had, and she had a feeling this woman may have them rather than some book on the shelf.

"I'm sorry. I shouldn't intrude. I'm just very interested in this subject. I'm Cathy, by the way!"

"Nice to meet you. I'm Susanne. You're new to the area? I haven't seen you before."

"Yes! I moved here with my husband several days ago because he got promoted. We're living on Sun Avenue in Bradwell."

"Oh, that's nice!"

But there was that tell-tale flicker in her eyes again, the twitch of her lips as though her facial muscles were tiring from the strain of forcing herself to smile. Cathy's heart beat slightly harder and faster too. Did Susanne know about the house and its grim history?

"It is. Was. It's kinda why I came into your shop. I, umm, think the house is haunted."

There, she had said it. Cathy felt a little embarrassed saying such a thing to another adult, but at the back of her mind was that threat, the warning, hearing the whole house rumble like an earthquake was occurring right beneath their feet.

"Oh. Well, I have several books on the subject you might like to take a look at. For instance, this one here, it's—"

"Susanne, I don't think a book is going to help us in this case. Not unless it's a report on unsolved murders in the area. I need real help, human help."

"Oh. I, umm, don't know what to say. My shop is more about reaching out to one's deceased, finding peace in the wake of a death of a loved one. I'm not sure I—"

Susanne was obviously startled. More than she should be. Cathy thought she would have been incredibly curious to know what was going on in her home, how she might be able to help, but the impression Cathy was getting was that this woman wanted her to leave right away. She was already walking back to the counter.

"Susanne, I'm in desperate need of someone's help. I thought you might be able to help. Someone I could reach out to. I dunno, a priest even if it comes to it. There's something happening in my home, and it needs to be stopped. There was a brutal murder took place there a couple of years ago. Two young children and their mother. The father disappeared. They don't know if he killed himself or fled. But if I don't help them, they're going to harm me and my husband. They've already told us they would."

Susanne but appeared to be debating something within herself, chewing her lower lip and frowning. Cathy waited for her to say something, her breath caught in her lungs. She somehow knew Susanne had more knowledge of such matters than she was letting on. Her demeanour was a giveaway. This woman probably spent more time speaking with the dead than the living.

Another customer walked in. Cathy's heart dropped. This was surely the moment when the customer was a lifelong friend of Susanne's and they would spend hours chatting away, Cathy's problem already forgotten about.

"Hi, Susanne! How are you today? You look better!"

"Janet, Hi!"

Oh no. I knew it.

But then Susanne did something totally unexpected. After they were done with formalities and a brief chat, Susanne smiled at Cathy and turned to her friend.

"Janet, I'm sorry. I'd love to chat, but I have something important just come up. I'm going to close for an early lunch."

Janet left. Susanne flicked the sign on the door to closed.

"Come sit with me in the back. Tell me what's happened."

Surprised at the sudden change of heart, Cathy followed her into the back, a small room dotted with candles and incense sticks. A table with three white candles in the centre sat in the middle. It made Cathy wonder if she was some kind of medium. Her heart beat faster. Could she have been so lucky already?

"Tell me what happened," said Susanne as they both sat down.

She told her everything except the fact the spirits were blackmailing her over her abortion. For now.

Susanne continued chewing her bottom lip, the inside of her cheeks. Something obviously bothered her, but Cathy had no idea what. It was starting to scare her. Was this something even more dangerous than she originally thought? Should she start looking for an exorcist or something outrageous?

"I remember reading about that," she said eventually. "Terrible, horrible things that must have happened to that family, yet the fact none of the bodies have ever been found was the most horrific, I think. Apparently, we now have some possible answers. Someone came to me shortly afterwards, a police officer who was investigating the case. Asked me if I could somehow contact them, tell him where they were, but I declined."

"So…so what, you're a medium or something? You can actually contact the dead? Oh my God, I really need your help. I have no idea where to even begin looking. Could you try? Come to my house, see if you can speak to them."

Susanne shook her head. "No, that's not possible. I don't do that anymore. I lost the ability, sorry. But, as to your concerns, no, spirits cannot physically harm a living person. But as you've probably already found out, from what you've told me, they can make life hard. I'm curious about the wailing baby, though. Maybe the mother was pregnant when she was killed. That would explain it; otherwise, I don't get it."

Shit. Do I tell her or not? What will she think about me? She's probably dead against abortions. Of course she is. She used to be a medium. But she was getting desperate. If she could somehow convince her to use her ability again, it could solve everything straight away.

"They've told me that I have to find him. Him I assume to being the father, whose body was never found. But I have no idea where to look. If the police couldn't find him, what chance do I have? And if I don't, they…they'll do things. They've already left little warnings. A few years ago, something happened my husband doesn't know about. But somehow these spirits do, like they can read my mind or my memories, and they've been leaving little hints. He mustn't know, it's imperative. I'm desperate, Susanne. Each day that goes past they're getting angrier. Please."

Susanne said nothing but picked at her fingernails, refusing to look Cathy in the eye. But the longer Cathy waited, her breath barely escaping tight lungs, Susanne's featured changed. It was as if she was having a silent conversation with herself, weighing the options. Her lips were thin gashes then blossomed, as though preparing to kiss someone. Her eyes wide then squinting; she shook her head, nodded, shook; little sounds came from her, sighing, tutting. Cathy was fascinated despite her desperation; she would have sworn she was in a heated argument with someone. Finally, Susanne looked up at Cathy.

"I'm sorry. I can't. It doesn't work for me anymore. I suggest you try and contact the spirits yourself. Ask them for more clues if they're that desperate for you to help them."

She rose from her seat, waiting for Cathy to do the same. The conversation was over.

Chapter 17

If things could possibly get any worse than they already were, this would be the one thing on the top of Cathy's *Cannot Possibly Happen* list. Especially now with everything going on, the spirits in her house threatening to reveal her darkest secrets, putting her marriage and her whole life in jeopardy. There was absolutely no way she was prepared for this, if ever. She had discussed the situation plenty of times with John, and they had both agreed to wait, which was absolutely fine with her. After the last time, she thought she might be happy waiting until she was dead.

There was a good chance it was just nerves. Hell, perfectly feasible it was her nerves, especially after being turned down by Susanne earlier that day, just when she thought the woman was going to agree to come to her house, speak directly with the intruders in her home and solve everything. Yet no matter how much she pleaded, Susanne stubbornly refused. So it was down to her, and she still had no idea how to go about resolving the issue.

And now this.

She had spent the better part of the afternoon either preparing dinner, looking over her shoulder every five minutes half expecting to see three ghostly apparitions glaring and looming over her pointing accusatory fingers, or running to the toilet to throw up. She had considered nerves, of course, or that she had eaten something off, but she knew the sensations in her stomach had nothing to do with that. The only time she had felt anything remotely similar was when she was pregnant. And now that feeling had returned.

She and John had always taken precautions, but there was the remote possibility they failed. It seemed that was exactly what had happened. In the worst possible moment. She had debated with herself all afternoon about running to the nearest pharmacy and buying a cheap pregnancy test, but with the luck she had been having lately, what if she bumped into someone there? The next-door neighbour who just happened to walk in as she was paying for it and might, just might, decide to congratulate John the next time they saw him? Things like this happened all the time; it would be just her luck. The pharmacy was less than five minutes from her house.

And wouldn't it be better to just pretend it wasn't happening and then it might magically go away? She considered this same possibility when pregnant last time, that she would wake up one morning and the foetus inside her would be gone—no more worrying, no more pretending it was something else that caused her moods to suddenly change, that all the throwing up was due to having eaten something rotten. No more lying to John.

But no, there was no way she could handle a suspect pregnancy on top of everything else occurring around her. Tomorrow, first thing, she would go to the pharmacy and grab a test, to hell with the neighbours. She would like to have a chat with them anyway, ask them to explain why the hell they lied to her about the previous owners.

When John came home that evening, she forced herself to eat the large steak she had made—John's favourite, which was another sign of her guilty conscience—as she told him about meeting Susanne and her refusal to help.

"Go to the police station," he said. "Maybe they have information they didn't release to the press. That's usually the case with unsolved murders. Perhaps the detective who came knocking on the neighbour's door knows something. Especially if he went to this medium asking her for help. He probably believes in ghosts so might take you seriously."

That was another good idea, something she would do tomorrow straight after begging the little contraption to come up negative. Fortunately, there hadn't been any sign of the spirits all day—maybe they were giving her a little reprieve to do what they asked of her. Allowing her a little respite over the fact another disaster was brewing in her belly.

She lay in bed later, barely able to keep her eyes open, while John took a quick shower. She imagined that thing inside her now, barely the size of a peanut, and having to explain to John why she was feeling so nauseous lately. He would probably be delighted; he had, after all, occasionally mentioned to her that whenever she was ready, he would be there for her. He had also hinted that if she wasn't ready for kids yet, then maybe she should return to studying. Staying home alone all day couldn't be healthy. Study, go to the gym, make friends. Do something, in other words. And he was right about that, but how was she supposed to make friends when living in the home of a coldblooded killer, now convinced all the neighbours were gossiping behind her back?

Does she know the truth yet? You think she's related to them; that's why they bought the house? She hasn't even bothered to introduce herself to anyone yet—must be related.

Something else to think about when all this was over. If it ever ended. She grunted when she felt the bed move and John climb in beside her. *I must have been drifting off, after all. Not surprising, I guess.*

His hand stroked her hair as he leaned over and kissed her. She smiled. He smelled fresh, like a newborn ba—no, don't think that, she told herself. That problem is being fixed tomorrow. She had done it once, she would do it again. She giggled as his fingers tickled her chest, fingers running over her breasts so lightly they might have been feathers.

"John, behave. It's late and I'm tired. You just woke me up as it is. Go to sleep."

He groaned, long and drawn out as his fingers caressed her tummy, then the palm of his hand lay flat on her stomach. It made her nervous. He never did that; he knew not to bring back unwanted memories.

"John, stop," she said, picking up his hand and squeezing it. "Go to sleep. Tomorrow, I promise."

"Talking in your sleep again, honey," said John as he walked in through the bedroom door, dressed in just his underwear.

Cathy bolted upright, a scream bubbling away in her throat. She dared to glance to her left. The bed was empty.

Chapter 18

As soon as John left for work, Cathy jumped out of bed and got dressed, quickly tying her hair in a ponytail, not wanting to waste a moment. It had taken a lot of persuasion on John's behalf last night for her not to sleep in the spare bedroom or on the sofa. When she had told him someone had been in bed with her and she thought it was him, at first a grin had worked slowly across his face. But when she burst into tears, he quickly jumped in beside her and held her tight. She had never felt so terrified in her life, something so utterly creepy. That hand, which it turned out had been an imposter's, gliding over her breasts, resting a palm on her tummy. It had known about the possible pregnancy, just as it had known about the abortion and was, what? Warning her? She had nearly thrown up all over the clean sheets thinking about it again, that long winded groan, kissing her on the cheek. It was the last straw.

She rushed downstairs to make herself a coffee, if only to allow herself to wake up a bit more so the people in the shops didn't think she was some kind of addict, but refrained from breakfast. No way in hell that was going to stay down today. As soon as she poured herself a mug, she sipped at it, ignoring the stinging of her lips and burning of her chest as it reached her stomach, and forced the rest down. A check in the mirror in the downstairs toilet showed only mildly bloodshot eyes, which was plenty good enough. She left Sparky's food bowl full and headed off to the pharmacy.

Fortunately, she didn't come across the neighbours or anyone else she recognised as she paid for the contraption. Even so, she threw it in her handbag and left quickly. Her heart was racing as she arrived back home and went straight to the toilet. Again, even as she waited for the results, she felt the common symptoms that would be confirmed any second; her breasts were sore, her stomach as though she had eaten something that might have been in the bin for the last few days, and an overwhelming desire to burst into tears and sob her heart out.

Cathy stared at the thing in her hand. It was impossible. Some cheap thing made in China that didn't work properly. She shook it hard, glared at the information on it, and waited a little longer.

Negative.

A sob burst from her mouth as the relief threatened to drown her. She leaned back on the toilet seat and closed her eyes, thanking God and everyone else that mattered for proving her wrong. But...the symptoms. If she wasn't pregnant, what was it? She knew those damn symptoms; she had been through the exact same thing first time around, and it wasn't just her nerves, feasible as it might be.

There was only one thing to do. On her way home from her next mission, she would stop off at another pharmacy and buy another kit. If it showed negative as well, she would have no choice but to consider taking something for her nerves. And they weren't going to abate until she solved this ghostly, gruesome mystery. So, taking John's advice, it was time to go to the local police station.

She had another coffee, this time to calm down her thudding heart so the officers didn't think she was coming to confess a crime, and applied a light coat of makeup. If they were going to take her serious, the last thing that would help her case would be her looking like she just spent the last three months in Northgate Hospital for the Mentally Impaired. She had driven past that place the other day, and shivers had run through her body. If she didn't figure this thing out soon, she guessed she might find herself there for a lengthy spell.

She arrived at the station, a small place, almost overlooked, which fitted the idea of a small village constabulary. It was only the small plaque beside the door that gave away its presence, and for a moment it made her wonder what these people were going to be able to do to help her. Surely, the most serious work they did was arresting the odd drunk now and again or rescuing cats from trees. And yet, she also knew from doing her research that Bradwell and the surrounding villages boasted their fair share of horror. Not least starting with the house she was currently living in.

Cathy took a deep breath and stepped in.

She had written down the number of the detective that had spoken to Susanne, but somehow this didn't seem the kind of place that housed detectives. Surely they were at a much larger station that dealt with serious crime, but she was here now, so she was determined to at least speak with someone.

The desk sergeant was a guy overweight and looking to be near retirement, too, judging from the worn features and wrinkled skin. He looked up, semi-interested, as she approached, no doubt expecting a complaint about her mobile phone being stolen or annoying neighbours playing their music too loudly.

"Hi. Umm, I was hoping to speak to a Detective Winters."

"About?"

"Umm, an incident a couple of years ago at the house I recently moved into. On Sun Avenue."

The desk sergeant squinted as though trying to recall if the road sounded familiar or not, and after a few seconds he looked up at her suspiciously.

"Do you have any information on what occurred there?"

"Sort of. Not really. I just wanted to speak to the detective in charge of the case. It's quite important."

He continued staring at her for a while, perhaps trying to decide if she was wasting his time or not or if he should arrest her now. "Hang on," he said after a moment. "I don't know if he's here or not."

In other words, go and find him and tell him there's a suspicious-looking woman at the entrance. He sauntered off to the back of the station and knocked on a door. He stepped in and spoke to someone while at the same time glancing back and eyeing Cathy. A couple of seconds later, he was joined by another man, dressed in a grey suit, and both headed back to the desk, the plain-clothes officer coming around the side to greet her.

Cathy was surprised to see he, too, appeared to be in his late fifties. Receding grey hairline, red nose and cheeks that suggested he was either permanently cold or enjoyed a little sip more often than not, and he was plump, his stomach craning over the belt of his trousers. His hazel eyes were kind, though, although she guessed this was a double-edged sword when it came to getting results. Instead of smiling as he approached her, he assessed her with something akin to curiosity.

"I'm Detective Winters. You asked to see me?"

"Yes. Umm, is there somewhere we could talk privately?"

He raised his eyebrows and led her to another room. The station was a lot bigger than it looked from the outside, rooms branching off everywhere. Several uniform and plain-clothed officers sat at desks typing, chatting to each other or on phones. They all glanced her way as she walked past, making her feel far too conscious. She wondered if, when she left, they would all be laughing at her behind her back.

Detective Winters invited her to sit down in what she guessed to be an interrogation room, cold and bare except a table, a recording device, and a camera in the opposite corner.

"So, the desk sergeant said you have some information about the case on Sun Avenue?"

"Umm, sort of. I understand you were the detective investigating the murders that took place there?"

"Yes, I was. Namely, finding the bodies of the victims and potentially the husband and father. Why? Not haunted by them, is it?! Or you found their bodies in the basement?"

A shiver of doubt ran down Cathy's spine. The man was grinning at her. If she said yes, would he even let her finish? Maybe he saw her doubtful expression, because his grin rapidly dwindled. But she had to give him something or he wouldn't tell her where they had looked for the husband and what they had achieved so far.

"I spoke to a friend of mine I met recently, Susanne, who runs a little shop selling stuff related to the afterlife and so on. She told me you'd contacted her about trying to reach out to the victims, see if they could tell you where the husband might be."

"Yes. I mean, it was a long shot. I don't really believe in this stuff, but we had no leads, no clues as to his whereabouts or whether he was even alive. But I'd heard she was quite successful at contacting spirits or whatever you want to call them, so I tried. Why?"

"Well, I only found out about what happened there by accident. If not, I might not have bought the house, but…But, since we moved in, we've been hearing things. Seeing things."

He must have remembered his earlier joke because he now looked sheepish and surprised. He sat up straight then leaned in closer, as though they were sharing some secret between them.

"And what, exactly, have you seen and heard?"

Here goes nothing. Northgate Hospital, here I come.

"The two children and their mother. I—we—have been seeing their spirits. They've been leaving messages telling us to find him. We assume they mean the father, either where he is or his body. And if we don't, they're…they're going to make things difficult for me."

"Difficult? In what way? Why don't you just leave?"

"We can't leave. We only just moved in and all our savings went into buying and decorating the house. My husband is going to work in a rented car because we don't have the money to buy a new one yet. We came from Peterborough. We're completely new to this area. As for making things difficult, they've been getting scarier. When we first moved in and thought it might be haunted, we laughed about it. I thought it was quite romantic. I saw this little girl now and again. I mean, ghosts can't hurt people, can they, so yeah, we thought it was fun. But now…they've been threatening me, that if I don't find him they'll make life tough for us. I was already scared shi…witless last night, and I don't know what else to do. I was hoping you could tell me what you dug up about the missing father or what clues you had, what you thought might have happened so I can help find him or his body."

There, it was out. In her mind, she could already hear the steel door of her cell at Northgate clanging shut, trapping her inside forever, her arms tied across her chest in a strait jacket. She waited for the inevitable chuckling to begin, to be told to get out and stop wasting police time, but instead, none of that happened. Instead, Detective Winters sat back in his chair and stared at Cathy passively, tapping his pen on the table, making her even more nervous.

"What?" she said finally, unable to withstand the silence any longer. "You going to arrest me for wasting police time?"

"No, I'm not. As I said, I'm not a great believer in these things, but that doesn't mean to say I don't believe at all. You strike me as being an intelligent person, not prone to making stuff up like that. And to be honest, after what we found at that house, I'm not too surprised their spirits want a little justice. I would too."

"So you're gonna help me?"

"That's the trouble. There's not a lot of help to give. That's why it's a cold case. We found three pools of blood in the main bedroom, presumably from those living there. DNA results proved they were all members of the same family, but four people lived there. Our guess was that the husband killed his family and committed suicide, but we have no body. Our next assumption was that he fled, but despite all our efforts, he hasn't been located. There's a good chance he left the country, but Interpol has had no luck finding him either. It's as though he vanished into thin air.

"The fact you say you've been seeing the mother and her two kids' spirits suggest the pools of blood belonged to them. And yet, a thorough investigation has brought no results whatsoever so far. No money taken from his bank account, not a single possible witness has come forward to say they may have seen him. So I'm afraid there's not a lot I can suggest. What exactly did these spirits say to you?

Didn't they leave any clues or hints as to where he might be?"

"No. Only to find him. But I don't know if they mean his body or his whereabouts. The fact they want him found to me implies he's still alive somewhere, but where?"

He shook his head. "As I said, we exhausted every possibility. He may even be dead somewhere for all we know. I'm sorry I can't help further. But why don't you ask Susanne to help—that to me seems the best bet?"

"She refuses. Says she doesn't do that anymore. That she lost the ability or something, although I don't think she was completely telling the truth."

Never had Cathy felt so dejected and helpless. This had been her last shot, her only idea into finding the father, alive or dead, and this detective was as clueless as she was. It meant going home and waiting for the wrath of the spirits and for John to discover her secret. It was down to begging Susanne, as the detective suggested, or finding a way for the spirits to give her more clues. Either way sounded like disaster.

Chapter 19

With Cathy out shopping, John was left alone in the house. It was a rare day when he could work from home, which under normal circumstances he would have appreciated. But these weren't normal circumstances, and he was finding it difficult to concentrate. Even though the cat wasn't allowed in his office, it had somehow found its way in, curled up on a chair and fast asleep. He didn't have the heart to wake him up and throw him out. He also had the constant, unsettling feeling someone was watching him from somewhere in the room, causing him to spin around quickly to try and catch them. That, plus casting glances at the cat, which he was using as a warning sign; if the cat suddenly jumped up and started hissing, he would have further proof he wasn't alone. The constant spinning on his chair was making him dizzy.

But this was the lesser of his problems, although he guessed that could change at any moment given the situation they were in. Right now, what worried him more, something that was far less supernatural, was his wife's behaviour. She was acting strange, stranger than perhaps she should be, ghosts or not in the house. He could understand her being edgy and nervous—hell, he was too—but her behaviour went beyond having a ghost jump out at her or scribble riddles on the wall. What happened to her in bed the other night had scared him too—the idea that one of those damn apparitions had been in his bed, caressing his wife…that was just sheer fucking creepy. He thought he might have gone and slept in the garden had it happened to him, so he was pretty proud of her for listening to him and staying. But for how long?

But that wasn't what bothered him. What did was seeing how she absently ran a hand over her belly all the time, as though she was pregnant again. The way her moods changed for no reason, and how on several occasions he found her muttering to herself while rubbing her belly like she did before, gently speaking to the foetus inside her. It made him wonder if the ghostly wails they were hearing occasionally was affecting her subconsciously, bringing back the memories of that terrible time. And for that he could never forgive these ghosts in his house or understand their own tragedies.

Just yesterday afternoon, they had been sitting on the sofa, absently watching a movie, and he had seen Cathy rubbing her belly, tears dribbling down her face. He had been tempted to ask her what was wrong, put an arm around her, but at the same time he didn't want to bring up the subject in case he was wrong. She had sat up, glancing around the room, her eyes squinted as though straining to hear something only she was capable of. But the way she was acting also reminded him of when she had been pregnant the last time.

It was only when he insisted something was wrong with her, she was acting weird, prone to bouts of sudden sobbing then eating the strangest of foods, she had confessed she was pregnant. And John had been delighted, not able to understand why she was so upset, as if she had been cursed instead of blessed. She refused to talk about it and spent some time at her friend's house, leaving John totally mystified. It was a few days later she said she had had a miscarriage.

And here she was acting exactly the same as before.

Yet that was impossible. They took all the precautions necessary; starting a family was not something they wanted right now, at least not until he was firmly established at his new job. Surely it was whatever these spirits wanted from her that was making her act this way. Regardless, it needed to stop soon or Cathy was in danger of falling ill again like before. Might have to go back on her meds for a while.

He stared at the plans of the site he was helping to construct on his laptop, but he might as well have been staring at a toddler's drawing—lines and shapes blurred until it was an incoherent jumble.

He thought of just grabbing Cathy the cat and taking all three of them to some cheap hotel until they figured a way to make the ghosts disappear—call a priest, anything. Burn the house down and hope he could cash in on the insurance so soon.

He glanced back at the cat, still purring in his sleep, not a care in the world except getting fed each day. Such a simple yet perfect life. Maybe one day he would come back as a ca…

John looked at the screen. His plans had disappeared, replaced by what amounted to nothing more than a squiggle. As he stared closer and mapped out the scraggly lines, he realised they were letters. And when he thought back to the fridge magnets, he saw the same word scribbled there—KARL. While he was trying to think of anyone he might know called Karl, the cat hissed behind him, making him jump. John spun around to see the cat standing up, his fur on end, tail bushy and prominent, and his gaze focused on the hallway past the door, looking ready to attack someone at any second.

"Sparky? What is it? What do you see?"

He looked back at the screen again. The word KARL was scribbled all over it, flashing in bright red letters. From somewhere in the house, a distant wailing started, a toddler or baby crying. It seemed to come from everywhere and nowhere. From behind the walls, beneath his feet. He slowly rose from his chair, feeling the hair on the back of his neck rise too. It was such a haunting, tragic sound he wasn't surprised it brought back terrible memories for Cathy whenever she heard it.

The cat arched its back, ready to bolt or attack.

"Hello? Anyone there?" he called, immediately feeling foolish. "I can't help you, you know. I don't know what you want, so either tell us or go away. If you want our help, you need to tell us more."

The wailing grew louder, as though he was stuck in a room full of toddlers. He gritted his teeth, clutched his ears. "That's not helping!" he yelled.

A shadow drifted across the hallway. The cat howled and bolted underneath John's desk, cowering in the corner. The wailing was so loud it was making his teeth chatter, items on his desk to rattle. It was like a jet aeroplane was flying overhead, circling him, deafening him with its screeching engine. The shadow grew in length, and something thundered on the stairs, some giant creature clumsily coming down them and towards him with gargantuan feet. He backed away, knowing he was trapped unless he threw open the window and jumped into the back garden. He considered doing it, too, but he held on to what he told Cathy; ghosts can't physically harm you, only scare you. And right now, they were achieving just that.

The shadow morphed into the outline of a human, growing across his carpet like an oil stain until it was inches from his office door, then stopped. From the ceiling came dripping. Bright red drops splattered onto the black form, first slowly then faster until it resembled a scarlet waterfall cascading down onto his floor. But instead of spreading over the floor like a puddle, the huge drops began to take shape, as though covering some invisible form and giving it a visible presence. The thing continued rising until it was nearly John's height—a grotesque, red, dripping human outline. Finally, the cascading ceased.

The blood dripped down the figure's outline and disappeared into the carpet, leaving behind it a semi-translucent outline of a person. Two arms reached out to him, a head cocked unnaturally sideways so its ear was resting on a shoulder. He saw no clothing or any distinguishable marks on it, just a foggy outline, the front door visible beyond. And yet its stomach was grossly bulging as though heavily pregnant. A sobbing wail came from its mouth, echoing the toddler earlier that had since stopped. Its arms dropped to its belly and caressed it, then instantly, as if on cue, a dark red substance seeped from between its legs and ran down them, while at the same time the bulging stomach gradually decreased in size.

John had no idea what he was looking at, yet at the same time knew exactly; the thing was imitating a miscarriage. Cathy's miscarriage. He wanted to cry, plead for the thing to stop and go away, leave them in peace, but all his muscles were frozen in place except his bladder, which cried to release its contents, so terrified and distressed was he. As the last drops had ran down its legs, the shape now a lean thing, wailing and howling once more reverberating around the house, the thing reaching out for him again and its dark, cavernous mouth opening wide.

"*Find him!*" It screamed so loudly John was knocked to the floor, as if its words carried a weight with them, driven into him from some vicious gale.

Then everything went silent, and the figure disappeared. Only when the cat dared to creep out from his hiding place did John dare to rise. And headed straight to the bar for a stiff drink.

Chapter 20

As before, Cathy knew she was dreaming but was powerless to alter the course of her actions or make any decisions. It was as if they were being made for her by some cosmic entity watching over her. She drifted from her bed where John lay snoring gently and muttering to himself, then turned and stared at him. A smile formed on her face as she contemplated how much she loved him and all he had done for her. She guessed that if she insisted on returning to Peterborough and escaping this godforsaken house, he would drop everything in a heartbeat. She hoped it didn't come to that, though.

Outside, an owl hooted to its companion or loved one. Another answered its call. The moon illuminated the room, high in the sky directly outside the window as though watching her with its silvery iris. A cat screeched, making her jump. Then something else screeched, this time coming from inside the house. At first, she assumed it was her own cat, perhaps replying to the other, imitating the owls with their haunting speech, but she knew that wasn't the case. She was being called by another being, something lingering in her home, using her secrets to communicate with her. Its marionette.

Her legs obeyed, and she turned to the bedroom door and headed out onto the landing. Sparky was sitting at the bottom of the stairs looking up at her, his glassy eyes like twin planets floating in the abyss. The way he sat there, motionless, unblinking, unnerved her. What was he thinking? Waiting for? Was he beckoning her, enticing her to head down to him, perhaps lead her to a trap?

Regardless, his hypnotic stare worked, for she began to descend the steps, their eyes locked. When she reached the bottom, he hissed and bolted. She chuckled despite him making her gasp. He was playing. She hoped.

The basement door swung open, hinges screeching like the cat outside. Down there was an even darker abyss, like the entrance to a black hole, all light swallowed up making it impossible to see the bottom or even the steps leading down. It might have led to the centre of the Earth for all she knew, walking down and down for all eternity until she reached the gates of Hell. But wherever it led, whatever was down there, her feet took her in that direction anyway. As her bare feet touched the first wooden step, it creaked ominously. Something shifted in the dark below.

Even though she couldn't see a thing, she somehow knew where she was going, knew exactly where to place her feet so she didn't get some nasty splinter stabbing the soles of her feet, knew exactly when she reached the last step. Ghostly whispers echoed around the room and in her head like a breeze was passing through. Something brushed her hair that might have been a cobweb or the gentle caressing of fingers. She flinched, spun around, and saw nothing. Something tugged her hair, causing her to spin around again, still seeing nothing.

She was disorientated, unable to recall where the stairs were, but it didn't matter because she wouldn't be allowed to return to her bed until they were finished with her. Whatever that may be.

A steady dripping began, as though there was a leak in the roof. If that was the case, they were huge drops because they splashed onto the concrete floor like grenades, the sound ricocheting off the walls, giving the appearance of standing next to a waterfall. A pungent, coppery smell came with them that assaulted her nostrils, like she was in John's garage as he worked on their car. She took a step forward, and when she raised her foot, a squelching noise accompanied it.

Then came the sound of scratching, as though someone was frantically raking fingers down brickwork. Whimpering followed as someone blew into her ear, whispering her name. Cathy took another step forward, her feet almost glued to the floor, struggling to lift them. A finger ran down her naked back causing goosebumps to rise like mushrooms on her arms.

"Where is he?" was hissed into her ears from both sides and in front of her, and she could feel cold, stagnant breath on her face. The breath of someone who hadn't brushed their teeth in weeks and had been living on a diet of rotten meat. She gagged and tried to turn away, but it was all around her now, smothered by a toxic, spectral cloud. Cathy yelped as she was pushed forward, struggling to stay on her feet but inevitably crashing to the ground, creating a loud splash as she connected. Only able to see and not feel it, her body was now soaked in a thick, warm substance as she tried to push herself to her feet again. It was as though she had sunk into quicksand, requiring all her strength to break free from the sticky prison she found herself in, slurping and squelching following her every move.

"Where is he?" came the ghostly chorus again. "You promised."

"I tried!" she wailed. "I need more. Where to look. Is he alive or dead? Tell me and I can help!"

As she pulled herself up, she was flung against a wall. Hissing and whispering rose in pitch and volume, appearing she was surrounded by people, hundreds, all screaming into her ear at the same time. A baby began to howl right in front of her as a pinching sensation began in her stomach, causing her to double over, and she knew that baby wailing was her own, lost two years ago.

"Please!" she begged. "I can't help without more information. Tell me where to look!"

The pinching to her stomach, as though she was being prodded by dozens of needles or knives, abruptly stopped and she was pushed forward, crashing against another wall. She spun around as a great, piercing scream reverberated around the dark room, making the walls shake, and then the grating rake of nails down brick started again, as if a dozen people were desperately trying to claw their way out from some hidden room.

Slowly, as though someone was gradually turning the button on a light switch, an orange glow provided a murky illumination to the basement so she could see vague shapes around her, as if walking through a dense fog, everything ghostly and faint. But for some reason, only a small area was visible, the rest as black as it had been before. As she tried to take a step forward, her arms outstretched to feel her way around, shadows slithered across the floor, eerie forms dashing past her, accompanied by wails and screeches.

"Please!" she begged again. "Tell me where to look!"

She stopped when her body abruptly collided with something solid. She felt around and scraped her nails along the familiar roughness of bricks. Panic fluttered its wings in her stomach, and she tried to find a way out, the only light visible a tiny square she could look into the basement through.

She was trapped.

Somehow, she had walked or been pushed into some hidden room, and it magically bricked itself up behind her. She banged on the wall, screaming to be let out, while silhouetted figures continued dashing past her, too fast to determine their identities although she already knew who they were.

"Please, let me out! I promise I'll find him, but you have to let me out now. I'm claustrophobic!"

She was answered by taunting chuckles, a boy and girl. As Cathy peered through the tiny gap, the size of a missing brick, three figures appeared before her. The mother and her two children. All three stood before her, expressions solemn and desolate, their faces and bodies marked by multiple gashes and deep cuts that still oozed blood, running own their legs and pooling on the floor. The three simultaneously tilted their heads as if contemplating or studying the woman behind the wall. Their outlines, barely silhouettes, flickered, the grim orange glow of the room like a setting sun, making them almost inconspicuous.

"Please, just tell me where to look. I want to help you, but I need more information. Is he alive or dead? Is it his body you want found or your own? Your remains? Let me out and we can find him together."

The three lifted their heads then quickly glanced to the left as if disturbed by movement. They turned back to her, but now their mouths were wide and gaping, as were their milky, white eyes, perfect representations of terror and shock. Three arms rose and pointed at her. The dripping returned, and now she could see it for what it was, although she had already known—her body was still coated in the dark crimson gore. It ran down the walls—her side—and dripped onto her face and into her eyes. She wiped them, trying to ignore the stinging sensation as she continued begging them to help her. Another shadow appeared to her left, much bigger than the others. It stomped across the floor, causing the walls to shudder.

The three spectres were more agitated, their semi-translucent outlines flickering as though seen through an old film reel. The two children looked especially terrified, clinging to their mother desperately. A roar echoed around the basement like some huge carnivore in terrible pain, stomping ever closer. And then the mother and her two children disappeared abruptly, and all went utterly silent.

Cathy was about to plead for them to return, to let her out. She was going to try and kick the wall down despite being bare footed. She didn't care if she broke her toes—she couldn't stay down here forever. But a new shadow and an aura passed across the floor, emitting a sensation of utter rage and hate, something she could feel and taste on her dry lips. As though a heavy raincloud was hanging over her, carrying with it all the world's loathing and revulsion so it was a solid, tangible thing that was going to unleash itself upon her at any second.

Two fiery red eyes appeared inches from her own, alive with scorn and iniquity.

A repulsion, thick with malice and contempt, oozed from its eyes, alive like roaring flames. Its skin barely hung on, dripping from its face like melting candlewax, exposing the raw flesh underneath. Something resembling a grin or snarl appeared, showing black gums and rotten teeth, the tongue now a decomposing blob. And as it glared at her, Cathy knew who it was.

The father.

His face pressed against the opening, blocking out what little light there was. Cathy stumbled back from the foul stench he gave off, the heat from his eyes enough to melt his flesh. He glared at her for an eternity, saying nothing but whining and growling like a cornered feline.

"Go away," she whimpered, yet at the same time she wanted to ask him where he resided, what foul domain he had taken as his own that his wife and two children were so desperate for her to find, but the utter terror he was instilling in her only made her wish for him to disappear.

He might have sensed it, too, because he started chuckling, a sick, croaky chuckle that sounded like his throat was filled with some horrible, thick liquid. And maybe it was, because he began to drool from the corners of cracked lips, thick like snot, dangling from his chin before plopping onto the floor.

But something, a last vestige of determination that resided within her, forced her to approach one step closer, knowing this was her chance, perhaps her one and only, to find out where he was.

"Where are you? Tell me where to find your body."

He stopped chuckling and turned serious, his eyes boring into hers, perhaps reading her thoughts and memories just as his family knew how to read her secrets.

"Who said I was dead?" he growled then raised his hand, something large sitting in his palm. His grinned returned as he showed Cathy the object he was holding.

"No! No, no, no! Stop!" she screamed as the thing placed the brick in the gap, locking her in darkness.

Chapter 21

Susanne was on edge. Fidgeting constantly on the sofa, trying to read *The DaVinci Code,* she found herself reading the same paragraphs over and over and the words not sinking in, failing to form coherent sentences in her head. She was grumpy, too, the slightest things annoying her, which was uncharacteristic for her. The neighbour outside her house revving his car engine made her want to go out there and scream at him to turn the fucking engine off. When the postman came and knocked a little too loudly for her liking, she threw the door open wide and asked him if he was trying to break in or just deliver the stupid, damn parcel. She slammed the door in his face when he left, horrified. When she made herself a salad and had forgotten to add salt and olive oil, she was too annoyed with herself to return to the kitchen, so she left it untouched on the coffee table in front of her.

It was the same feeling as when she craved a cigarette from when she was younger, hating herself for smoking the disgusting things yet at the same time willing to do anything to obtain a nicotine hit. It was also the same feeling as when she felt she was shirking from her responsibilities. There were people out there that desperately needed her help, yet she was deliberately making excuses both to herself and those in need to avoid doing so. She had never taken drugs, except nicotine, but she imagined what she was feeling now was similar to what a junkie felt when needing another fix. No matter what she did to take her mind off things, it didn't work. Her mind returned again and again to the Soul Searchers, as though they were her children that had gone off to live faraway and she hadn't seen them in years. And in a way they were. She had adopted them, not to replace Sally but as a reminder of her. When she went more than a couple of weeks without seeing them, her heart ached.

But as well as being smitten with her ethereal friends, was she also a glutton for punishment? The image of the creature in her mind still haunted her, the way it had destroyed the last house she had visited, almost killing her in the process. She still walked to and from work each day keeping an eye out for Dennis should he suddenly appear with a big knife in his hand.

And in a way it had killed her, because an important part of her had died that day, the part that got her through the lonely nights, sometimes wishing she was with Sally in heaven, sometimes wishing she had never been caught in time for the blood to stop flowing from her wrists. It was helping others who had been through a similar fate. It was something she could relate to more than anything else, and it had been taken from her. To continue would mean a fate worse than any blade to her wrists or lost soul roaming Earth.

She thought she had tricked herself into believing she truly had stopped using her abilities and could continue until her dying days from using it ever again. But the despondent look on Cathy's face the other day when she had come to her shop, begging and pleading for her to help, had opened fresh wounds, these not on her wrists but in her heart and soul. She had cried after Cathy left, both for the woman and for herself, but there was no way she could risk the wrath of whatever dark spirit roamed that world for a third time.

Susanne picked up her book again, tried to read the next chapter, then after just a couple of minutes threw the book down in disgust. She got up, poured herself a glass of wine, and tried to settle down and browse Netflix, but nothing piqued her interest. Every time she found a series that looked like it might be good, she would forget what was going on within ten minutes. All she could see was a picture of a distraught Cathy in her mind, imagining what she and her husband had to be going through. Not one but three entities haunting her, demanding she resolve the mystery they seemed incapable of resolving themselves. Surely, a brief visit wouldn't hurt, just a quick look, see if she could help in any way but without resorting to calling the Soul Searchers?

Don't do it, Susanne. Remember what happened last time. Don't get involved.

But if she didn't, that fidgety, anxious sensation would not go away. It *was* a drug, who was she kidding? Never since learning she had the ability and how to use it had she been more than a few days from that parallel world. This was the longest yet, since the previous time she had come face to face with the darker forces that resided there also. And besides, this was completely different. She didn't really need to contact the Soul Searchers; the spirits demanding attention were there in that house. She could contact them there. For Susanne, it would be as easy as chatting to a neighbour.

Wouldn't it?

Soul Searchers

She arrived at 17 Sun Avenue thirty minutes later, a perfectly normal road, quiet with the odd few coming home from work. It was nearly seven pm, and the sun was already beginning the slow yet inevitable journey down past the horizon, replicating her own downwards trajectory, or so she believed for she couldn't quite believe she had succumbed to her inner calling once again. But she told herself for the umpteenth time she was just paying a quick visit, just to get a sense of whatever might be occurring within its walls.

Some glanced her way as they strolled by, while men and a few women looked her up and down, either admiring her figure or the bright, hippy dress she was wearing that reached down to her sandaled feet, wrists and neck covered in bright artisan jewellery glinting in the fading sun. It was something of an irony that she preferred to go unnoticed in the world yet at the same time dressed so that never occurred. Those that knew her recognised her from impossibly long distances.

She stood across the road from the house, not wanting to bring any more attention to it, still amazed all those that walked past completely ignored it, as if its notoriety was something they preferred to elude or pretend had never happened. Considering the grisly events that took place there, she half expected dozens of kids to be goggling at its windows, hoping to catch a glimpse of some elusive ghost.

A flicker of a curtain in the upper right window caused her heart to flutter. She waited with bated breath for some horrific face to appear there, perhaps acknowledge her presence, but instead, Cathy's long, black hair waved as the woman passed by the window.

The poor woman, what she must be going through, living in a house knowing there had been such brutal slayings there. She didn't think she could have done it herself, and she was used to dealing with all matters of the occult and supernatural. Susanne was about to cross the road, try to pick up any aura the house might be giving off, when there was further movement from the left upper window. She could still see Cathy moving about in the window opposite, perhaps doing household chores, so she assumed it was her husband. Maybe it was his office up there.

The figure was nothing more than a shadow, backdropped against the setting sun so it was impossible to tell, but she was pretty sure he was staring at her. She hadn't met him, so perhaps he was wondering who the hippy woman was staring up at his house. She waved and smiled so he didn't think she was some crazy sightseer. He waved back but still didn't show his face. To his right, Cathy closed the curtains, then seconds later the light went off in the bedroom. But her husband—if it was him—remained in the shadows, perfectly still as if a shop mannequin left by the window.

It was starting to make her feel uncomfortable, as if he was hiding in the shadows on purpose, not wanting to be seen or recognised. If that was so, why had he acknowledged her presence? She thought of entering the garden and knocking on the door, but an instinct, a warning in her heart, told her to wait.

Now others were glancing her way, too, seeing her standing there for so long and doing nothing except stare at that bedroom window. She noticed them glancing up as well, as if there was something extremely interesting going on—something naughty and explicit perhaps, and now she was conscious of everyone looking at her. She thought of leaving, returning tomorrow or not at all, and was about to do so when the figure shifted, edging slightly closer to the window.

The world around her darkened at the same time, as though a large cloud had obscured the vanishing sun, preventing it from offering one last peek at the world before departing. A cold breeze brought goosebumps to her arms, and she wrapped her cardigan tighter around her. A shadow descended on the house like a growth, casting it into an eerie darkness, yet none of the other houses on the row were affected by it, remaining as bright as before. The figure in the window took another step closer, now barely inches from the glass. She strained to pick out any features, then suddenly found herself being dragged towards it, her feet acting of their own accord. There was a screech followed by a blaring car horn as a car to her left abruptly hit the brakes. She screamed, tried to jump out the way as the driver furiously yelled and insulted her, but she was powerless to do even that, her legs continuing across the road, oblivious of any oncoming danger.

Susanne tried everything she could to break the mental grip whatever was controlling her had on her, reaching out to the Soul Searchers despite swearing not to do that again, but her mind was blank, as if some invisible chain was dragging her towards the house. When she reached the gate, it swung open of its own accord, clattering against the small, brick wall. Her body was forced left onto the garden. When she was in the centre, she stopped, her head craning up towards the window as if she was seeking divine intervention.

Which she was.

She tried to scream for help, for Cathy, but only a pitiful whimpering came. The curtains parted like the Red Sea, exposing the shadowy figure whom she now knew wasn't Cathy's husband. The whole world was like a dense fog, spectral shapes moving around her, impossible to determine their identities, only a distant humming moving slowly towards her. Faint screams and wails reverberated in her head, long lost souls desperate to find their way, as was she. And then it appeared.

A thing so hideous and grotesque she wanted to curl up and die looked down at her from the window. A shape constantly morphing into something else; first, some giant, multi-eyed creature, like a fly or spider; then into the corrupted shape of some bulbous, gelatinous creature, an octopus, perhaps, with two huge, golden eyes like blazing fires and multiple tentacles swinging behind its head. A mouth, vast and gaping, stretched impossibly wide, showing rows of needle-sharp teeth like some prehistoric monster gnashed together, instantly snapping upon impact to be replaced by newer, larger ones. Her head felt as though its mouth was feeding on it, biting off great chunks—resounding throbs and stabbing sensations in her brain burning up in her skull.

"*Get out!*" boomed a voice in her head, the force of which impacted her mind so strongly that she nearly went flying across the garden. The thing's eyes—once again multiple like a spider—glared down at her, burning with such an intensity the glass began to melt around it.

"*Get out or die!*" came the voice again, and this time Susanne's limbs loosened and she bolted, crying in terror, not stopping until she reached her home and bolted all the doors and windows.

Chapter 22

Cathy sat in the living room on the sofa, nursing a steaming mug of coffee and holding a sleeping cat on her lap. She found it ironic that upon moving in it had been the cat that was first seemingly terrified of the house, while they found the notion of living in a haunted house romantic and fun. Now it was the complete opposite; the cat barely even continued with its incessant glaring at the basement door or ceiling in the bedroom. Now that the secrets of the house had been unveiled, it was as if the underlying terror that had accompanied them had, at least for the cat, disappeared, left only for Cathy and John to bear the full brunt of.

She took another sip of her coffee, scalding her lips and not caring. It meant she was alive, her body had not slipped into a complete paralysis as she feared it might after waking up late last night screaming. It had taken all John's strength to hold her down, prevent her from running from this cursed house and doing whatever it took to get back to Peterborough. She would sleep on her parents' sofa if necessary. It also took him considerable time to make her understand it had only been a nightmare, although considering how her previous nightmares had come true, that she had dreamt it was irrelevant. He had had to go to the basement himself, still in his pyjamas, and check there were no hidden walls down there. And even when he said there weren't, it was only because he was an architect and knew where to look for any tell-tale signs, she had slowly calmed down. She still had an overwhelming urge to burn the place down.

It had been so vivid, far too much to be a simple nightmare. The sounds of the wailing and screaming in her head, the smell of the blood and its stickiness as it clung to her body like glue. Her hands had been sticky when she finally came out of her hysterics, and she had to scrub them hard with soap and a stiff brush. And then there had been the father, glaring at her with those eyes of his and the stench of decay and rot that emanated from him like a broken sewer pipe. She could still smell it. And the utter darkness, like no other she had ever known, when the last brick was put in place, shutting her off from the rest of the world, condemning her to die through thirst or lack of oxygen. Every time she opened her wardrobe doors to grab something, she had to put a chair against them to prevent them from closing on her.

There was no way it could have been a simple dream as John insisted. There had to be some kind of meaning to it, not just the spirits telling her to continue with her impossible mission. And how they had managed to bring back either the father's spirit or a simple image they had somehow created she didn't know. If his spirit was hovering around the same realm as they were, in this house, why did they need her to find him? He had been right in front of their faces. They had done her job for her.

Thus, it could only have been an extremely vivid image of him they had made, perhaps as a clue, a warning, she didn't know, only that this was getting to be too much for her nerves to handle. The threat of a spell at Northgate Hospital was hanging over her like a guillotine, her anxiety at breaking point. What if they left another clue for John to find? Then it would be the end. She would have no choice but to go back to her parents, who would practically shun her—them and their religious, no-nonsense ways.

As for John, after what happened to him, he was spending less time at home too. There was no reason for him to be at the office every day; he could work from home perfectly well. But lately he was making excuses to get out. In a way, she didn't know if that was a good thing or not; at least he wouldn't be finding any more clues as to the baby's real father.

There had to be something she could do. She felt like the answer was tantalisingly close, within grabbing distance. The spirits needed her to do a job for them and surely were doing everything they could to help her. It was in their own interest, so why was she still clutching at thin air? In her dream, she had been walled up alive, the father cementing the last brick while his dead wife and children looked on. So, if he was dead, they would have been able to contact him themselves, deal with him however they saw fit in their world. Which meant…

"My God. He's still alive. He didn't commit suicide or kill himself, somewhere hidden where they couldn't find him. And more, he can't be far away either. If not, they would have left a message somehow last night," she whispered to the sleeping cat. As much as it stung her, crippled her soul to think about it, she ran through the events of her nightmare again.

The walls and floor dripping blood. The baby in their hands—her baby. Finding herself trapped in some hidden room. Him appearing. Who said I was dead?

That was what he had said before placing the last brick. He had said that through his wife and kids. It was a message, what she had been asking for.

The cat screeched as she jumped up, her heart racing in danger of overloading. Cathy grabbed the car keys and rushed out.

"I'd like to speak to Detective Winters," she said, breathless after bursting into the police station.

The desk sergeant eyed her nervously as before, then slowly wobbled off to find him. There was a hopeful yet suspicious glint in the detective's eyes when he saw it was her again. Perhaps he thought she had returned with more fantastical details of ghosts and apparitions and was going to drag him down with her madness. Yet at the same time, seeing that grin on her face, he must also be considering she had finally found something tangible he could use to solve the cold case.

"Mrs Richwood, you're back. You got some more information for me?"

"Yes!"

He looked at her for a few seconds, then nodded and indicated for her to follow him to the same room as before.

"Okay, what have you got?"

"He's still alive."

"Who is?"

"The husband."

She told him about her nightmare, what the father had said, and waking up with her hands sticky and still smelling the man's aura. The sparkle in the detective's eyes faded.

"Mrs Richwood…"

"I know what you're gonna say, but it was real. As real as it could be, anyway, not just some vivid nightmare. They want me to find him. That was their way of telling me he's still alive. And he's close—he hasn't escaped the country or anything. I think he's still here somewhere, hiding. Perhaps using a false name. We can find him!"

"Mrs Richwood, even if what you say is correct and they really did manipulate an image of him to show you he's alive, we've searched for him for years. Even Interpol checked across Europe, and we have never found a single clue as to his whereabouts. Why and how would that change now?"

"But…"

Fuck!

There had to be something. He was here somewhere. Maybe they had been looking too hard for something that was right under their noses.

"But did you actually check Bradwell and the surrounding villages and towns? Maybe you've been looking too far, assuming he must be hundreds of miles away or dead. He could be living on the same street for all we know."

"And what do you suggest we do? Interview every single person who lives in the surrounding areas and oblige them to give us DNA samples? You have any idea how long that would take? What it would cost? All based on a nightmare that wasn't real."

Cathy slumped in her chair, defeated. She had been so excited that the real nightmare might soon be over, and in less than two minutes, this detective had crushed all her hopes. Because he was, of course, right.

"Listen, I can tell from your reaction you're disappointed. Probably desperate. I can't imagine what it must be like to live terrorised by ghosts. And I'm one of those who has an open mind to these things. I've had my own experiences in the past, but what I'm saying is if they're so desperate themselves for you to find him, can't they, like, leave messages somewhere if they know where he is?"

"But that's just it, I don't think they do know where, only that he's alive. I think they want justice served for what he did. Because if he was already dead, they would have no need to contact me. They could do it themselves."

"So you're convinced he's somewhere close," he said, more to himself as he scratched his stubbly chin. "Serial killers like to return to the scene of the crime on a regular basis, keep a check on whether the bodies have been discovered or not, see what evidence had been found if any. To the point they'd often join in the search parties. Perhaps this guy, Alex Hamshore, was doing the same—wanting to be close to the scene to keep tabs on how the investigation was going. But any possible suspects we had—which were a lot—we took DNA samples from, no match. It would have been a man his age at the time—forty-two—recently moved into a flat or house on his own but with a new passport, driving license, social security card. But then how would he have been paying for his new lifestyle? He had to have a job somewhere. Somewhere no one would recognise him. Bradwell was flooded with police officers, journalists, you name it. So unless he had plastic surgery as well…

"Listen, I'll have another check. See if anything has come up lately. People arrested with false documentation. But I can't promise anything. I'll have to do it in my own time, as well, which will take longer. But if I find anything, I'll let you know straight away. Just…I dunno, try and get these phantoms to give you more information."

Cathy's hopes were deflated once more. The detective working on his own in his spare time, that could take weeks. By then, her own life could be over and it wouldn't matter whether they found this man or not. She thanked him and left, dreading the idea of returning home alone again, wondering if the spirits of three desperate people were waiting for her, ready to finally give up on her and reveal to John that her baby not only had died from an abortion instead of a miscarriage, but that the father's name had been Karl.

Chapter 23

Cathy wasn't home when John returned early from work, making him uneasy. After calling her name repeatedly and hearing nothing, he briefly considered going to the bar for a drink, go window shopping, back to the office on the pretence he had forgotten something. Anything so as not to be alone in the house. But then he reminded himself Cathy was here alone all day every day, and that thought made him feel like a wimp, a coward. Besides, being afraid to be in one's own home was not how things were things were supposed to be. The complete opposite, in fact.

But the scene in his office the other day had scared him badly. He would never admit to Cathy, but the idea of fleeing this damn house and running back to Peterborough was something that had crossed his mind on numerous occasions. Every time he opened a door or even sat on the toilet, he expected one of those ghosts to appear again, that terrible wailing to start in his head, for something to happen to make him scream like a little girl. But he had to be strong for Cathy. She was the one who was suffering the most. These spirits were drawn more to her than him, and he had the idea they were threatening her somehow. Something was driving her mad with worry, but he didn't know what it was.

He had thought of driving to the local church, speaking to the vicar about getting the house blessed or casually enquiring if exorcisms were such a thing anymore, but when he mentioned it to his wife, she had said no, it didn't work like that and wouldn't make any difference anyway. When he pressed her about it, she refused to indulge him, saying it was down to her and her alone.

Right now, according to her text message, she was at the police station talking to the detective who investigated the case. He didn't know what she hoped to achieve there, but she was trying her hardest to figure this mystery out. He hoped she did so sooner rather than later. Last night he had caught her rubbing her belly again and mumbling to herself. She had stopped wearing makeup, leaving a pale complexion to her face that made her look ghostly. She tied her hair back in a simple ponytail to avoid brushing it, and no matter what he prepared for supper, she barely touched it.

A couple of times he had tried googling more information about the previous owners with no success. All he could find was a generic message from the police saying that if anyone knew the whereabouts of Alex Hamshore to inform the police immediately, that he was wanted in connection with a series of brutal murders. But that message was from over a year ago.

It was all taking a toll on him too. He was worried about waking up in the middle of the night needing the toilet, too scared to rush down the landing just in case and thus incapable of getting back to sleep again for fear of pissing the bed, his groin a throbbing, constant ache. Cathy not in the mood to cuddle up to him at nights, and both were too exhausted to push the matter. The slightest creak on the stairs caused his spine to freeze. This could not continue. Whatever these stupid fucking ghosts wanted needed resolving before they both suffered nervous breakdowns or worse.

The majority of the activity seemed to occur in the basement. Cathy's nightmares always saw her waking up down there or were the setting for them. And when he had gone down there himself after she insisted he check for hidden rooms, there had been an unsettling atmosphere about the place. The air had been thick and charged with static as if some intense, terrible event had recently occurred there and its residue, the memory of it, was still clinging to the walls and floor. Twice he had nearly bolted up the stairs after seeing a suspiciously human-looking shadow in the corner that flickered and shifted, barely perceptible but enough to make him flinch.

He ran everything he knew through his head again. Three people died in this house, the fourth member of the family had disappeared, and their ghosts wanted him found and wouldn't stop until he was. That meant, as Cathy had said, he had to be alive, and their objective was surely justice for the horrible crimes he committed. And their bodies had never been found. Either the man had eaten them, which was unlikely, or he had buried them somewhere so well-hidden the police had been unable to find them, probably dismembering them in the process to make their detection even harder.

The clues were there; they just needed piecing together. But where to look?

John tugged the cord illuminating the basement in a dull, orange glow, reminding himself for the thousandth time to change the lightbulb that looked as though it had been there since the house was built. His heart thudded slightly faster, perhaps warming up in preparation for anything that might see John bursting back outside again. He took a deep breath as he scanned the bottom, as though getting ready to take on some impossible task. Sensing nothing except the clogged and feisty air that wafted slowly up to greet him, he cautiously headed down the wooden steps, part of him ready to turn and run should it be necessary. To where he didn't know, but he sure as hell didn't want to get trapped down here. Cathy could be hours in returning home.

He wandered slowly around the room, running a hand over the walls, looking for any crevices or erratic brickwork, anything to suggest something out of the ordinary; a loose-looking brick, a wall that that wasn't in keeping with the main ones. The boxes that were still piled up against one wall as though trying to hide something—that became the focus of his attention. This wall was part of an L-shaped area, no doubt built to hide the sewage pipes that ran down its middle. He pulled away the boxes and junk leaning against it and ran his hands over the bricks while scraping at the cement with his fingernails. If the murderer had decided to bury them in the house, this would be the place to do it. The difference in colour and texture from the bricks and cement would be visible. The house was over seventy years old—much of the original brickwork was already crumbling in places, and he knew as an architect that at some point a coat of cement would be required to strengthen them. But that was for later.

He banged on the wall, hollow as he expected. Surely the police would have knocked a few bricks out to check, same as he was doing? The floor was solid concrete, so there was no chance of the owner digging that up. So logical place, if he had indeed hidden the bodies, would be here. But nothing suggested that had happened. Then he remembered the neighbours' kid had said something about a hole near the bottom, so he got on his hands and knees and crawled along the wall, checking for air vents at the same time.

Nothing.

"Fuck," he muttered as he stood up again. Another dead end. He had really hoped to find loose bricks, something to indicate the wall had been tampered with recently. Then when he knocked a few out, he would peer inside and find three skeletons on the floor. At least then their remains could be properly buried, and this nightmare might be over. Or at least be passed onto someone else.

Not knowing what else to do, he headed back towards the stairs, thinking about checking the attic. It was a very small place and filled with even more junk, and the one time he had inspected it there had been no sinister smells assaulting his nostrils. So unless the bodies had been in tightly-closed plastic bags, it seemed unlikely they would be there either. But then, his back to the basement, he stopped. The hair on his neck pinged to attention, prickly and sending chills down his spine. There had been a change in the atmosphere, he could sense it. The air was more alive, as though a thunderstorm was heading his way, having formed just above his head. He shivered involuntarily, as though a ghost had run right through him. The temperature seemed to drop ten degrees. He considered bolting, forgetting whatever was right behind him, for he knew without having to look that something was there. He slowly turned around.

As if on cue, that haunting wail began, echoing off the walls, a baby hungry or cold. But this time, instead of it coming from all around, from behind the walls themselves, the baby, a tiny thing John could hold comfortably in one hand, was sitting in the arms of another, two young children beside her. But now, rather than being the mother of the two children, her ghostly presence shimmering and semi-translucent as before, it was Cathy's image that stood there, looking grim and sad.

He stood, both mesmerised and horrified by the apparition. The baby was a tiny red thing as though just born and hadn't been washed yet. Blood still dripped onto the floor from its limbs and face—too much blood for it to be normal. It writhed and struggled in Cathy's arms while Cathy herself was completely naked, yet her body as though it had aged thirty years, wrinkly and saggy, her breasts almost reaching her waist, liked deflating balloons. Her long, black hair was grey and bald in places, giving the impression of some huge cobweb covering her scalp.

Apart from the baby, all three stood there staring morbidly at John, expressions of despair etched into their bloodied faces. Long gashes ran across their throats, streams of crimson running down their bodies.

"Cathy?" he managed, barely able to speak, his Adam's apple caught in his throat.

Immediately, there was the sound of dripping, as though that thundercloud had finally unleashed its watery contents. But instead of rainwater, once more the walls turned red as blood gushed from between the bricks. And yet, rather than run completely onto the floor, words began to form on the wall, the blood defying gravity and travelling horizontally instead of down. Within seconds, the word KARL was written everywhere.

The baby stopped wailing and pointed at him.

John shook as though he had been slapped. Crimson tears ran down Cathy's ghostly eyes, her stomach began to swell as though being inflated. She reached out to him with both arms, the baby remaining in the air, also defying gravity. And then, as John was willing his legs to move towards her, hold her in his arms, her stomach exploded, showering him in grisly, fleshy shrapnel, her stomach now an open, flapping wound, like a portal.

Before he even had time to react, the word Karl flashed in his mind repeatedly like a neon beacon, and a flashback to when he first met Cathy came to him. She was talking to a guy in a bar, both giggling, staring into one another's eyes. He remembered now; the guy lived not too far from their home, an old schoolmate of hers. His name was Karl.

The second the realisation passed through him, the basement returned to exactly how it had been before. John remained there for several moments longer before slowly returning back upstairs. An idea was floating around in his head, and he found it very difficult to believe it was the ghosts playing tricks on him again.

Chapter 24

Cathy was nearly in tears as she stepped inside her home. She had hoped the detective would jump up, call his team, and immediately reopen the case, stopping at nothing to locate the whereabouts of the missing man. He had murdered his own family and was on the run; surely, there had to be specialised teams that dealt with these kinds of cases. But he had promised her nothing, not even attempting to get the case opened again.

Her anxiety and despair were at a breaking point. She felt sick almost constantly; sometimes just the sight of food was enough to send her running to the toilet. And even worse, her period was late. It should have come this week, but instead, when she went to the toilet there were seepages, just as before. Her breasts were painful to touch, and when John had done so the other night in bed, she had gasped, not in ecstasy but in pain. With everything going on, she had forgotten to go back to the pharmacy for another kit. As much as she wanted to deny the impossible, that she might be pregnant was floating before her eyes like a bad omen. If she was pregnant and then later John found out about Karl, what was she going to do if John left her?

To her utter dismay, John was sitting in the living room staring absently at the TV, his features pale, eyes bloodshot.

"John? You okay?" she tentatively asked as she kissed him.

He shook his head. "Where've you been? I was worried."

That simple comment eased the intense throbbing of her heart. That he was asking about her, telling her he had been worried, suggested he hadn't made the connection yet, that the ghosts hadn't revealed her secret. Maybe she still had time. She told him about her revelation that the killer had told her in her dream he was still alive and how she was convinced he was close by. How she had gone to see the detective, who had told her it was entirely feasible he was still in the area perhaps to maintain contact with the house and any fresh news that may come to light, but that the detective said there was still little he could do to help.

"I don't know what else to do," she said, nearly sobbing as she laid her head against his shoulder. "Who knows what these spirits will do if we don't help them. We need to leave, John. Get out of this place before something bad happens. We could stay in a cheap hostel or something, rent a room. I dunno, but it's getting worse. The nightmares. You look terrible yourself."

He snorted. "We have nowhere to go, remember? I don't even get paid until next week. We can barely afford to eat. Everything we had went into moving here.

"I checked the basement by the way."

"Really? Why?"

"After what you said about being bricked up, I thought there was a chance their bodies where down there, having been bricked up themselves, but I didn't find any skeletons. Not that, anyway…"

The way he ended his comment caused Cathy's spine to prickle with fear. He had seen something, but what? She could tell from the look on his face and the three empty beer cans on the coffee table. John only drank alcohol in quantity when he was stressed.

"So what, John? What did you see?" she barely whispered.

"Are you pregnant?"

The question stunned her. That was the last thing she expected to hear from him. She tried to think of anything that might have given him reason to suspect but could think of nothing.

"Wh…what are you talking about? Why would you even ask? If I thought I was, I would have told you."

"I've seen the way you rub your belly, muttering to yourself. You barely eat, you don't like it when I touch you. I've heard you throwing up a few times. That's how you acted the last time."

"Well, I'm not! Throwing up, nerves, muttering to myself? How do you expect me to act, John? I'm fucking terrified!"

"I know you are, so am I, but…I promised never to talk about the miscarriage again, or even kids, but…is there something you never told me? Something I probably don't know or want to know about either?"

Oh no. What the hell were these cryptic questions referring to? Had the ghosts told him already? Is that what this was all about? At some point while he was in the basement, had they appeared and told him? That would explain the pallidness of his skin, his eyes bloodshot as though he had been crying.

"John, I…I don't know what you're talking about. Did something happen earlier? You have another experience with the ghosts? They…they say something?"

"Remember that guy who was infatuated with you when we first met? Karl, I think his name was."

Cathy's heart froze. She made to try and remember him, as if that name hadn't been on her mind the last two weeks. "I think so. My old school friend? Yeah, why?"

"In the basement, those three ghosts appeared again. But instead of the mother, it was an image of you. Pregnant. Then your stomach exploded and the word Karl was scribbled all over the walls in blood. The word Karl was written on the fridge in the magnets, remember? It makes me wonder why. What are they trying to tell me?"

Cathy had no idea what to say. The idea one of the ghosts pretended to be her, and pregnant? Her stomach exploding and showering the walls in blood to spell that name? What the fuck was that all about?

It was obvious what it was all about. They had literally spelled out her secret to him, apparently forming an image of her pregnant as well, in case he needed more clues. It was as obvious and as clear as it could possibly be without one of the ghosts turning around and saying it to him.

"I...I don't know what to say, John. What are you implying? Why the fuck would one of them pretend to be me? And pregnant? I'm not pregnant, for fuck's sake! And this Karl, I haven't spoken to him in years. They must refer to my mother, I told you. But why, I don't know!"

"They spelled Karl, Cathy, not Karla. If they'd wanted to, I'm pretty sure they could have added the extra letter. I just...I don't know what to think. Was he the father of your baby? Is that what this is all about? Some secret of yours they're blackmailing you with so you solve their problem?"

"You fucking pig! You think I'd cheat on you with him? That ugly, spindly wreck of a kid? How dare you. That baby was yours, but if you're gonna start believing a bunch of fucking ghosts over me, then I'll leave. Now!"

She wanted to scream, run away, let the stupid ghosts rot in whatever constituted hell for them right now. She was doing her fucking best to help them, and this was how they were repaying her? Burn the house down, leave them in limbo forever, call an exorcist. But what she wanted more than anything in the world right now was to take back everything that happened to her with Karl. She had been drunk, it should never have happened, it was a mistake.

Soul Searchers

People made them all the time but didn't have to pay for it their whole lives. She wanted to wrap her arms around him, promise John it wasn't true, but she wasn't so sure she could look him in the eyes without betraying the truth. The man looked on the verge of tears again, staring absently at the TV, bottom lip quivering.

"John, I promise, it's—"

The basement door flew open and slammed against the wall, the hinges bending, a chunk of plaster falling to the floor. Wailing began, so loud they both screamed and covered their ears. John's empty beer cans shot across the room, while on the wall opposite them, two words appeared in what resembled blood.

Find him.

Chapter 25

Cathy awoke in the spare bedroom. She hadn't wanted to sleep apart from John, but she was determined to carry on the show of defiance against his accusations, and even though he had offered to sleep their himself, she had said no, she wasn't going to sleep in that room ever again. She was acting like a child throwing a tantrum, but it was all she could think of to continue the charade. John hadn't said anything else to her all night anyway; instead, he messed around with the basement door while drinking beer until he eventually gave up.

She climbed out of bed and listened for John's snoring, but when she heard nothing, she dared to peek in. He was gone. Probably woke up early himself to go to work and avoid her. Tears threatened to escape from behind bloodshot eyes once again. She felt dirty, a traitor, a piece of lying scum married to a man she didn't deserve. Perhaps she should tell him so he would finally be rid of her and find himself a real woman, not a liar and cheater.

But instead of that, what she was going to do was insist on finding the answers to the spirits' demands. Especially now that she knew he was alive and very probably in the area. She wasn't going to let them ruin her marriage just because they wanted her help and were blackmailing her into doing so. Once she found their killer, they were going to somehow pay for what they had done too. Hell, she would have happily tried to help them without the blackmailing, so she didn't know why the need for it. Maybe they had tried with whoever lived here long before they arrived and that person or family had run screaming in the middle of the night.

"Why are you doing this to me?!" she yelled at the empty house as she entered the kitchen to make coffee. The cat bolted, no doubt sensing trouble, yet nothing else moved or answered her.

"I'm doing my best, but I need more! You didn't have to tell my husband anything! That's not fair! I would have helped you anyway, you cowards!"

Where were they? Why didn't they appear and justify their actions? She poured herself a coffee as she waited, hoping for a reply, an apparition, anything, but as before, nothing came. She took a sip of coffee and her stomach tightened, almost causing her to drop the mug. It felt like someone was squeezing her intestines. A spout of nausea overcame her, and she bent over the sink, waiting for the bile to spew forth. After a few seconds, nothing came up, and she poured her coffee down the sink in disgust. Her period still hadn't come, and now this was terrifying her as well. Just as John was on the verge of discovering her secret—if he hadn't already convinced himself she was lying—there was the chance she was pregnant. And the irony of the matter was that this time it would be John's and he might not want it.

Cathy returned upstairs, dressed, then fed the cat before leaving, casting a quick glance around before leaving as if saying goodbye for the last time. And if she didn't find what she needed, it may well be.

###

The familiar tinkling of the bell above the door as Cathy stepped into *Heavenly Treasures* alerted Susanne to her presence, as before hunched over the counter reading a book. Susanne's smile was quickly replaced by a frown, her lips tightened to a thin gash, as she recognised Cathy.

"Hi, Susanne. I—"

"Look, I really am sorry about what you're going through, but I already told you I can't help you. I don't do it anymore."

But Cathy wasn't going to be dismissed as easily this time. "He's alive. The father, the man who killed his wife and children. They told me. He told me. Sort of like a vision of they conjured up while they locked me up behind a wall. In a dream, but it wasn't a dream. And he lives nearby, I know he does. All I have to do is find out where. You have to help me. They…they did something yesterday, basically gave away an important secret I have from my husband, and if I don't find this man, they're going to tell him the full truth anytime soon."

Susanne shook her head. "I don't know what I can do. Speak to the police, tell them what you just told me. Ask them to reopen the ca—"

"I did! I went there yesterday, and the detective told me there's not a lot he can do without more evidence or proof. I need you, Susanne. My whole life and future are being threatened. I'm being blackmailed by these things! They pretty much told my husband yesterday and now he suspects, and…"

She was on the verge of tears. She wanted to cry, but right now she didn't have time for such a triviality.

"But have you actually tried asking them where he is? I don't understand why they're blackmailing you, as you say. Why not just tell you where he is? And if they know this secret of yours, surely they must know where he's hiding."

"It's...different."

How could she explain that while they could probably read her thoughts, that didn't mean they could read everyone else's? Yes, it was in their interest he be found and quickly, but if they hadn't told her already, it meant they didn't know. She was going to have to tell Susanne the truth for her to understand the importance of finding him, what would happen to her marriage if she didn't.

A customer walked in just as she was about to tell her. She waited, flicking through one of the books for sale. It was about a woman's experiences as a medium. It might have been written by Susanne herself, she thought. Two weeks ago, she might have scoffed at what she was browsing; now, she was tempted to buy it, maybe try and contact the author. Finally, the customer bought some incense sticks and a magazine called *The Unexplained* and left.

"A few years ago, I made a terrible mistake when I'd just met John, my now husband. I was drunk, got to flirting with an old school friend, and got pregnant. I told John I had a miscarriage, but really I had an abortion. He still thinks that's the case. At least until now, because somehow these spirits know about it. They've been using this information against me to get me to find their killer.

"Apparently yesterday, they did all but reveal it to him, scribbling the word Karl—the name of the guy who got me pregnant—on the walls. It's not the first time. They're blackmailing me, and if I don't find this man, they're going to tell him straight. He already suspects. He cannot know the truth, Susanne. It would kill him. And our marriage. Oh, and did I tell you? I think I may be pregnant again. This time with John as the real father. I need this, Susanne. More than you can imagine."

Susanne stared at her as though she had lost her mind. Which wasn't far from the truth. Cathy didn't know whether to smile or burst into tears. It did sound completely surreal now that she had said it aloud.

"You're not joking, are you." It wasn't a question.

Cathy shook her head.

"Jesus. But...*blackmailing* you with this information? I have never heard of ghosts reading a person's thoughts or memories. It's technically impossible. And why blackmail you? Why not just ask you for your help?"

"We've been asking ourselves the same question. I would have happily tried to help. At first, we'd see this little girl running about the house, giggling then crying. We thought it was romantic and funny. Then things started happening. Maybe they thought we weren't taking them seriously, so they started leaving clues about Karl. They know their murderer is alive, but I don't think they know where. Only that he's somewhere close. Maybe even in this village."

"I understand now why you were so desperate for me to help. But…"

A dark cloud seemed to drift over Susanne's face. Her features tightened as though someone was stretching her skin. Cathy saw her shiver, the pen she was fumbling with in her hand dropping to the floor.

"What is it? Is something wrong?"

She looked like she had just seen a ghost. Or worse.

"No, it's…I'm sorry, I really would like to help, but…"

"But what? Why don't you want you to help me? All I'm asking is to try and contact these spirits. Ask them if they know where he is. Come to my house—you'll be perfectly safe."

"I came to your house the other day, Cathy, with that purpose in mind. But I saw something in the window. I thought it was your husband, but it wasn't. I can't go back there. There's…there's something dark and evil that lives in that world, too, and it won't let me. It will kill me if I do. Sorry, I think you should leave."

Cathy was stunned. There had been something at her window? Something that had scared the hell out of this woman, causing her to run off? But if Susanne had come to try and help them, why would they make her leave? It defeated the purpose.

Seeing as Susanne wasn't going to budge from her decision, Cathy mumbled a thanks and dejectedly headed home.

###

Cathy's eyes shot open. She looked around, momentarily disorientated until she realised she was in the spare bedroom, just a single ray of silver coming through the open window. She had had another bad dream, but this time there were no ghosts involved, no summoning her to the basement. Where she had been summoned, though, was just as terrifying.

Justin Boote

She had found herself standing before some huge building, the wide-open double doors beckoning her as though waiting to embrace her. She really didn't want to go in that place, it was giving off a terrible vibe as though the gateway to hell itself, but she found herself dragged towards it anyway. As she approached, her bare feet scuffed along the concrete path causing blisters to arise and audibly pop. She could hear distant howling, screaming, as though whoever inhabited this dark place was in great agony. Their wails of despair were abruptly cut off, as if something had been clamped across their mouths. The sounds of slapping and thudding followed.

Cathy was dragged into the entrance to the building. Spectral shapes drifted and floated along the long, grey corridors like wisps of smoke. At the bottom of the corridor, one wisp of smoke, tall and with more of a defined outline, motioned for her to follow. Against her own will, her feet obeyed. When she looked behind her, she saw her bloodied, blistered feet were leaving a slimy trail, like a giant snail. Bugs dashed out from their hiding places to lap it up, then were subsequently scooped up themselves by the wraith-like figures and swallowed whole.

She didn't know where she was but somehow knew she was in a madhouse, an asylum of sorts, which explained the wailing and what might have been the souls of its ex-inmates consuming the bugs. She reached the bottom of the corridor, turned right, and saw the silhouetted figure standing outside a door. This corridor, or ward, was full of cells—she could tell from the small view grids set in the middle of each door, groans and whimpering coming from inside each one.

She tried to resist, but she glided towards the figure regardless and stopped outside the door. It swung open. The stench of a thousand unwashed bodies assaulted her, coupled with the foul reek of a damaged sewage system as though the toilets were all overflowing and had been left this way for decades. Her eyes watered heavily, her throat as though something had gotten stuck in there, a bug perhaps, still squirming. Despite her utmost resistance, she was powerless to prevent herself from entering, then jumping as the door slammed shut behind her, possibly trapping her in there forever, just like the wall in the basement.

The walls, filthy and grimy, speckled with blood, grease, and what looked and smelled suspiciously like urine and faeces, were padded—another clue. The room was bare except for a metallic sink and toilet in the corner and a bed against the wall, a blanket—that might have been white a hundred years ago—as disgusting as the walls. There was a bulk in the middle of the bed, under the blanket, a chest slowly rising and falling.

"So you found me, then," came a gruff voice. "I knew it would happen someday."

"Who are you?" she asked, terror coming at her in waves, yet unable to move.

"You know who I am. Don't be stubborn and naïve."

It took Cathy a few seconds to realise what he was talking about. When she finally did, her heart inflated like a balloon, feeling like it pricked itself against her ribcage. The person she had spent all this time desperately looking for had finally been presented to her. All she had to do was pull back the blanket to identify him and understand exactly where she was. Her legs now free from whatever had been guiding them, she took a step closer, her hand itching to throw off the blanket and get a look at this monster's face. But when a gurgling chuckle came from under the bed, as if he was choking on some thick liquid, she pulled back again.

"What's the matter? Scared? What's wrong with you? If you don't look, you know what will happen; when you wake up, your husband will know your dirty little secret, you whore." He chuckled again. "Your life will be as fucked up as mine is. Fuck, you'll probably end up in a room yourself. Maybe we could share, like roommates!"

This time the bed bucked and rocked as he erupted into a fit of hoarse laughter, as that of a lifelong chain smoker. He was right; if she didn't solve this, tomorrow could be her last day as Mrs Richwood. She had no choice.

Cathy reached over again, grabbed the corner of the blanket with the tips of her fingers, and willed herself to tug it off. But she could already smell another surge of sweaty, decaying foulness drifting towards her as the blanket was raised slightly. Maybe whatever was under there was dead. All she would see would be a rotting, semi-decomposed skeleton, nothing but globules of flesh clinging to the bare bones. Maybe his eyeballs had sunken into crater-like sockets, glaring up at her with mischievous glee.

"Fuck it," she muttered and threw off the blanket.

The bed was empty.

She stood there a while, not quite understanding what she was seeing, waiting for her eyes to adjust to whatever they were failing to recognise. When nobody materialised in the bed, she squatted and looked underneath then slowly spun around, even looking up at the ceiling. He was gone. That raucous chuckling began again, but this time all around her.

"You can see me, but you can't!" he taunted. "I'm here but not here. Find me, Cathy. Come and find me. Before they hurt the baby. If you dare!" That last sentence roared into her head so loudly she screamed.

And opened her eyes in the spare bedroom.

Chapter 26

John sat in his home office, the door closed, staring at his laptop. As before, the symbols and words on the screen were a blur, a cloud drifting across his computer like the thoughts drifting through his head. Once again, Cathy had woken up screaming in the middle of the night with talk of the killer having visited her in her dreams again, but this time from whatever place he was currently residing at. A hospital or prison perhaps. Despite the fact they had barely spoken the last couple of days, he had comforted her, and she had allowed him to do so. It broke his heart to see her like this, but at the same time his heart was already darkened with pessimistic, nefarious thoughts.

It seemed the message these damn spirits were trying to tell him was so clear, clearer than what they were trying to convey with Cathy and the hunt for their murderer. He knew perfectly well it wasn't just nerves making Cathy act this way, although he was sure it contributed. She was pregnant. The woman had acted exactly the same way before, and he guessed not only was she scared about what these ghosts might do to her, she was probably terrified about losing the baby again and didn't want to admit to him she was pregnant to get his excitement up. And yet, there was something else going on he didn't quite understand. All this about Karl and babies, wailing and ghosts whose stomachs exploded as though pregnant themselves.

He hated himself for it, but the seed of doubt had been planted. Never since they had officially become a couple had he suspected Cathy of being the type to sleep behind his back, and much less with that prick, Karl, but what else could it be they were trying to tell him? What Cathy had said about the word spelling her mother's name was a mistake—she hadn't spoken to her mother since they moved in, and that was just to confirm they had arrived safely. So what could Karla have to do with all this?

Nothing.

Could it be they were trying to provoke another miscarriage in his wife, or at least threaten her with the possibility of it? That seemed far more likely. Hadn't he seen a movie or something once where the exorcist or priest had told the victim that ghosts and demons liked to play on their fears? Create fear and confusion before finally taking them over for whatever purposes they had? Maybe that was what the ghosts were doing—emotionally blackmailing Cathy into finding their murderer quicker so they could rest themselves. And yet, it still didn't answer all the questions he had, namely Karl's relation to all this.

If they were trying to install doubt in his mind, they were doing a pretty good fucking job. He had virtually accused her of being unfaithful yesterday, and she had responded by vehemently denying it then insisting on sleeping in the spare bedroom as though punishing him. And what had happened? She woke up screaming at the top of her lungs again. Then yelling something about a hospital. Well, there was further proof; dreaming about hospitals meant she was starting to think again about her miscarriage now that she was very probably pregnant. And if he insisted on trying to help her, she would refuse like the last time. When Cathy had phoned him in hysterics to say she had lost the baby, he had cried himself, telling her he was on his way to the hospital right now, would be there within minutes, but strangely enough she had told him not to.

"What do you mean, don't come?" he has asked her. She had just lost their baby, of course he wanted to be there with her, but no matter how much he pleaded with her she said no. Her parents were with her and that was all she wanted right now. Her parents whom she barely spoken to and who John would have said were the last people on Earth she would want near her in that moment. She had ignored him for a few days after as well, saying she wasn't in the mood for company and needed some time to herself to process matters. And despite saying it was his loss as well, she would not relent. He had been upset and hurt at the time.

And now, with what was going on, it made him wonder.

As far as he was aware, most of the activity seemed to come from the basement. That, coupled with Cathy's nightmare about being walled up alive down there, made him think if he was going to get any more answers from these spirits it would be down there. But going down those steps again was not something he really wanted to do. Ever again. He had been scared shitless last time and had, in fact, vowed never to go back again. But his curiosity was getting the better of him. And as they had both agreed from the very first time, the ghosts didn't actually hurt them physically, just scared the hell out of them. So what could go wrong?

John rose from his chair and headed purposefully yet uneasily towards the basement. After slamming open yesterday, it wouldn't close properly anymore, so he swung it open and tugged on the switch. He half expected to find the floor drenched in blood and gore again, ready for him, but it was quiet down there, not a sound or movement. He went down and stood in the middle of the room.

"Anyone here?" he called out.

Immediately, there was a gust of cold, mouldy-smelling air that blew past his face. Shuffling or what might have been scratching came from behind the wall. And then, from around the corner, a little girl stepped into view. Barefoot and wearing filthy, torn pyjamas like the first time, she walked past John, ignoring him as though he wasn't there, sobbing to herself.

Her long, blonde hair was matted in clumps, dangling over her pale face like strands of rope. Her pyjamas were splattered with blood, especially down her front, and her cheek had a long, deep gash across it like a demonic grin. Her back to John, she began scrabbling at the wall he had searched the other day, slowly at first then more frantically, whimpering as she did so.

"Hey? Can...can you hear me? We're trying to help you, you know, but we need more information. Can you tell us where your father is? My wife is trying as hard as she can to find him, but we need to know where he is."

The girl ignored him completely, her fingers now bloodied from torn fingernails. It seemed there was a purpose to what she was scratching, not just random as if in panic, desperately trying to claw her way in. Her fingers were running both horizontally and vertically, and he could now determine the letter K clearly in her blood. He watched, fascinated at what she was scribbling and horrified at her condition. There was nothing to suggest she wasn't real; she might have been some poor girl living rough and abandoned in the wild.

The letter A appeared next, and he knew she was going to spell Karl again. If only he could get her to tell him the meaning behind it all.

"Hey, I know you're spelling Karl. I know who he is too. But why are you telling me this?"

She finished writing KARL then slowly turned to face him. She looked like a corpse that had recently been dug up. Her skin was a mottled grey colour, cheekbones pushing through flesh that was stretched and taut, causing little slivers of skin and flesh to fall like snowflakes. Her body was skeletal, her rib cage poked through her chest, and her legs were so thin and twisted they resembled twigs. She grinned at him, and John grimaced when he saw blood running from between her legs, pooling on the floor.

"What is it? What are you trying to tell me? What is it about Karl? Why is there blood running down your legs? Did your father do that when he murdered you?"

Instead of answering, her mouth opened wide as though yawning. Blood ran from that, too, as she rubbed her stomach in a circular motion as if hungry or rubbing her belly like Cathy used to when pregnant. Is that what she was doing—imitating his wife?

"Is this about Cathy? She's pregnant? But what does that have to do with Karl?"

A grim chuckle came from the apparition, deep and hoarse like an old man's, blood still trickling down her chest. A red stain appeared at her belly, slowly growing outwards. Wailing came from her—a baby's haunting cries.

"She's pregnant, isn't she? But is it someone's else's baby? Not mine? That's what you're trying to tell me?"

The girl turned and started scratching at the wall again with both hands. He watched, barely breathing, his heart throbbing like a mad thing in anticipation of finally learning the truth.

A shadow appeared at the top of the stairs.

He jerked, the shock surprising him when he spun to face whoever it was.

"John? What are you doing down here?"

It was Cathy.

He turned back to the girl, wanting to show Cathy what was going on, that perhaps she would have some explaining to do, but she had disappeared, nothing to indicate she had ever been there.

Chapter 27

Cathy still didn't believe John's excuse about looking for some tool he needed in the basement. The look of shock and surprise had been too evident, then he had stumbled over his words as he offered an excuse. No, he had been down there looking for more clues or evidence, perhaps trying to summon the ghosts to tell him what he wanted to know. Which made the revelation she had received last night even more urgent. The father of that family was in a hospital or prison somewhere, she was certain. It was just a case of finding him which, assuming he was now living under a false identity, wasn't going to be as easy as she hoped.

While John was at work in his office with the door closed, which suited her fine, she opened her laptop downstairs in the living room and googled the names of all the hospitals in the area. There were two within a thirty-mile radius, one of which was a children's hospital, so she ignored that one. But how she was going to get private information she wasn't sure. Then she had an idea.

"Hi. Umm, I was wondering if you could help me," she said to the receptionist. "I'm calling from the Midlands. I was told a friend of mine who lives in Bradwell might recently have been admitted to hospital. I'm trying to clarify if it's him before I make the long journey to come and visit. An old schoolfriend. We were, umm, more than just friends for quite some time before I moved."

"Of course! Give me his name and I'll check the records."

"Well, that's the thing. It's been such a long time I can't remember his surname. His first name is Alex, about forty perhaps, and I know that he lived alone so probably won't have any visitors or anything, which might seem unusual. Do you have anyone called Alex there that hasn't received any visitors at all?"

She heard the clatter of keys as the receptionist typed something into her computer. Cathy waited, her breathing laboured as her heart throbbed in her chest so forcefully it seemed to stop her lungs from working properly. After what seemed an eternity, the typing stopped.

"I'm sorry. We do have an Alex here, but he's eighty-two, and another Alex, but his wife is with him right now. He's listed as being twenty-seven."

"No, that's not him. Do you have anyone who might have been

admitted recently with no next of kin or anyone to inform of his admittance?"

More typing on the computer followed. "No, sorry. Only a couple of elderly men and women, nothing that matches your description. Sorry."

Shit!

Cathy threw her phone on the sofa beside her. She knew it had been a long shot, but she had still hoped to have found him. A wave of nausea rose up, and for a second she thought she was going to throw up on the floor. She took deep breaths, waited for it to pass, then googled the nearest prison. Getting information from there was probably going to be impossible, but she had to try.

She received the same information.

There were no prisoners matching that age who had no visitors or contacts with the outside world. It was possible the father had remarried or had a girlfriend completely unaware of his past, but somehow she didn't think so. It was still too recent; he would have been paranoid about being discovered still. And considering what he had done, she had the idea this man must have a foul temper on him. At some point, his new girlfriend would have discovered for herself. The articles she had seen on the internet stated that Hamshore had been a builder. There were dozens of construction sites all around the surrounding villages; she would never find him that way. Not in time, at least.

So if he wasn't in the local hospital or prison, where the hell was he? That dream had been another premonition, an insight, she knew it as much as she knew she was indeed pregnant with John's child. Her period should have been and gone days ago, and her breasts were constantly sore and achy. Now, at the worst possible moment, she had once again fucked up. How was she going to tell him? Could she even bring herself to do so? Especially if he found out the bitter truth of her past. She thought of her friend suggesting she have an abortion. Cathy considered the idea briefly, knowing it would once again resolve an unwanted problem, but if she did, the knowledge she had willingly killed not one but two human beings would crush her. She might as well join the ghosts making her life impossible right now.

So before telling John the news, she had to first prevent him finding out about her secret. If he had witnessed something in the basement earlier, there was every reason to believe they would present themselves to her too.

"Please, I know he's in a hospital somewhere. I dreamt it last night—a vision. Give me one last clue as to which one. Please," she called out when she reached the basement. "You must know."

She waited, desperate to hear a sign, anything from them, but as the minutes ticked past and her desperation grew in intensity, she considered they were never going to tell her. Instead, they were going to punish her by revealing all to John, as she was sure they had been doing this morning.

"Come on, for fu—"

Faint scratching came from behind the wall. The one she had dreamed being bricked up in. As she listened, it became louder, more frantic, and now there were more than one pair of hands raking the brickwork.

"Hello? Can you hear me? Can you help me?"

The familiar wailing sound started—a baby sobbing intensely. And then, from around the corner, the mother appeared, shuffling along, her head down. She ignored Cathy and faced the wall, her back to her, then began raking at the walls.

"Hey, it's me, Cathy. Are you going to help me? Please stop doing that. I saw him, I know he's in a hospital somewhere. Do you know which one? I'm so close to finding him, and then you can be free. Get whatever justice or revenge you need and move on. Isn't that what you wanted?"

The ghostly woman stopped raking at the wall that was now smeared in blood from her torn fingers and slowly turned around. Cathy gasped. Not at the peeling, flaky, grey skin or the holes in her face where the flesh had already decomposed, or even the milky-white eyes. It was the huge bulge in her stomach from where the wailing was now coming from. The apparition raised a skeletal arm and pointed at her while rubbing her belly with the other.

Cathy watched horrified as her belly started moving, something squirming in there, trying to kick its way out. Cracks appeared in the mottled skin, like a bird breaking free from an egg. Blood ran down the woman's legs. She knew what was being said, insinuated—Cathy's abortion. Or what she had told John—a miscarriage. Or, she suddenly realised, maybe they weren't letting her know their intentions of telling John her long held secret. Maybe it was a sign the baby she was carrying inside her now wouldn't make it to birth either. Maybe, as retaliation, it would die as would their hopes of justice.

"Why are you doing this?" she said, careful to avoid John hearing her from upstairs. "Don't you want me to fucking help you or not? I should burn down this fucking house and let you rot forever here! Let's see you find your husband then!"

The wailing grew louder, as did the scratching on the other side of the wall. The ghost's mouth opened wide, and a shrill cackle came, like a crow. Desperate, furious, unable to cope any longer, Cathy looked around for something to throw at her. She didn't care if it went right through her or not, she needed to vent her anger and frustration. This was it; she was going to tell John she was pregnant and they were getting out of here. John's parents were dead, so they would go stay at her friend's house in Peterborough if necessary. Or John's office.

She glanced upon a large sledgehammer leaning against the opposite wall. Through sheer determination and adrenaline, she picked it up, despite being so heavy, and wielded it like an axe, almost falling over as she battled against the weight. Screaming with rage, she brought it down with all her force onto the grinning apparition, now not caring if John heard the commotion or not. As predicted, it went straight through her but dislodged a brick in the wall. She raised it again, repeated the same process while the dead woman just stood there, continuing to taunt her as the hammer went straight through her chest and hit the wall, causing two bricks to shatter and leave a hole. Still not satisfied, barely able to raise the sledgehammer above her head, she just managed to do so, and this time she let it fall from its own weight. Another two bricks shattered.

The spirit disappeared.

Panting heavily, Cathy dropped the hammer and leaned over, trying to get her breath back. After a few seconds of panting, she stood up straight and looked at her handiwork. There was a feisty smell of mould and rot coming through the gap. The sound of dripping water was louder as it ran down the sewage pipe in the middle of the bricked off gap. Now curious, she decided to inspect it closer, yet the thought of her nightmare and being bricked up in there was heavy on her mind.

She grabbed a torch and shone it around the small area.

And immediately jumped back in shock, the torch falling to the floor.

There had been something in there, reflected off the beam on the floor. At first she thought it might be the cat, just like her neighbours' kid said he saw. Cathy picked up the torch and shone it further in. Three skeletons lay there, one large and two small.

Chapter 28

Susanne hadn't expected to fall asleep so easily. She had expected to be staring up at the ceiling most of the night, unable to find a comfortable position, her mind wandering and lost. She had already drunk half a bottle of wine in an attempt to get to sleep quickly because her body needed it. Her mind needed it. It was as though a mental tug-of-war was going on inside her head; on the one hand, she was thinking of the desperate situation Cathy found herself in and wanting to help; on the other, she was remembering the warnings she had received several times now telling her to keep away. And she knew enough by now not to see them as empty threats by an entity that saw its realm threatened by an intruder, the possibility of losing its grip on the souls inhabiting it. The thing would kill her, and that would be the easy part. It was what would come later that terrified her even more.

Her heart begged her to ignore; her mind told her to run.

But her body didn't or wouldn't give up its incessant aches and sores, and her mind refused to forget the subject, allow her to sleep in peace under the pretence of it not being her problem. Because it was. It had always been her problem. Communicating with the deceased was what she had been put on earth to do, just like her mother before her and her grandmother before that. Helping lost souls move to the next plane. She felt empty inside. A large part of her genetic makeup had been swallowed up and spat out, leaving a hollow shell, the core of her now like roadkill rotting beside the road.

And she missed the Soul Searchers. She had heard them trying to contact her when she was drowsy at nights, her mind blank and finally free from horrific thoughts if only for a few hours. They knew the dangers, too, but it seemed they were willing to risk them, if only to say hello, let her know they were still there. She could hear their childish voices as she dozed off.

Finally, her body relented and she drifted into sleep. Almost immediately, she found herself standing on top of a hill. Far below, the river Waveney meandered past and beyond that, endless fields as far as the eye could see. The sun was shining bright in the sky, bathing Susanne in a warm cocoon of comfort and cheer. For some reason, she was extremely happy, happier than she had ever been, although she didn't know why. She shouldn't be happy; there were a million reasons why she should be aching with despair and grief. Everyone had left her. She was the last person alive on Earth or anywhere. Even the Soul Searchers had finally abandoned her, giving up on her weakness and cowardice, her failure to comply with what her body demanded of her—help the lost. So this must be some kind of punishment—condemned to roam Earth for eternity in utter solitude.

So why the happiness and cheer?

She might have been in Heaven, so perfect a day and scenario around her, birds singing in the trees to her left, deer and rabbits happily browsing close to her with not a care in the world. She thought that if she reached out, they would let her stroke them. As she strolled along the hill, tears in her eyes at such a profound beauty around her, wishing she could stay here forever even if she was alone, the ground beneath her darkened.

A sudden chill caused goosebumps to prickle her arms. She was only wearing a long, white dress, her feet bare, and now her whole body was cold as a strong wind picked up. The wildlife bolted in sudden panic. She looked up. The sun was blotted out by a single, dark cloud hovering deliberately in front of it, appearing as if by magic to ruin her dream; yet despite the strong wind, the cloud refused to move along.

Susanne shivered. The cloud, so black it looked like a solid thing, seemed to affect her mind, dampening her spirits, her body feeling twice as heavy as before when she had been practically floating along the grass. She could barely see in front of her now, a pitch black as though night-time had appeared at the flick of a switch, yet no moon sat in the sky.

Something or someone was watching her. The distinct sensation of someone following her from some secret location was too strong to dismiss. She looked around, calling out for whomever it was to show themselves. As if in answer, laughter carried along the wind; it might have come from someone directly behind her or at the bottom of the hill. And the tone of that laughter was something she recognised.

Fear gripped her. She spun around in circles looking for the owner of the voice, and at the same time, where she should run if necessary, yet all around her now were woods, appearing just as instantly as the darkness.

Then she heard another voice. This one was much more gentle, friendlier. Her name being sung to her, laughter. A break appeared in the black, and for a second, daylight returned. She briefly caught sight of someone standing further ahead, beckoning or waving at her. Then all was dark again as though night and day battled with each other for supremacy.

Whoever had been standing up ahead looked to be a woman or girl, slight in frame and long hair blowing behind her. Susanne moved towards the figure, while behind her loud thudding came as though something huge was stomping up the hill towards her. When she reached the figure, her fear abated and she smiled.

Sally was waiting for her.

They embraced each other, and in that instant, the cloud obscuring the sun dissipated and warm daylight returned once more. The booming, raucous laughter and the ground trembling beneath her feet with each step also disappeared, leaving the two of them alone.

"Where are we? What are you doing here?" babbled Susanne as she hugged her daughter.

Sally took a step back. Nothing suggested she was a ghost; she was as solid as Susanne was, wearing the last thing she had had on before her life was taken from her. Her beaming smile faded; she looked upset and serious.

"I came to tell you not to be afraid. The creature that lives in the other world is scared of you. That's why it keeps telling you to stay away, but you have to ignore it. Stay strong. Yes, it can hurt you if it wants to, but fear stops it from doing so. It was following you up the hill until it was aware of my presence. You mustn't give up; you're stronger than it is.

"The Soul Searchers are waiting for you. Go to them. Do what you were born to do; don't be afraid. They need you."

Susanne wasn't sure if her daughter was telling the truth or not. She knew full well how powerful that entity was—it wasn't just an empty threat telling her to stay away. She had seen what it could do before. But why would Sally lie?

"It's scared of you, Mummy. Remember that."

Sally slowly began to fade, waving as she left.

"No! Wait, don't go! I have so much to tell you."

But she was gone. As the tears fell, the world she was in became distorted and grey, as though she was in the middle of a dense fog,

Soul Searchers

until she found herself evaporating as well.

She opened her eyes to find herself lying in bed, but the sweet scent of that other world was still with her. Today, she decided, she was going to close the store for a while. She had other, more important jobs to do.

Chapter 29

John had his arm wrapped around Cathy's shoulders as they watched the medical examiner and his team walk down the basement steps. He kissed her on the side of her head and hugged her closer. Cathy responded, turning to look up into his face as though they were newlyweds. She couldn't be happier.

After discovering the skeletons in their grisly prison, she had dashed upstairs, yelling at the top of her lungs for John to come quick. Assuming something bad had happened, he almost ran into her as he came bursting out of his office.

"I found them! I found them!" she babbled.

"Found who? What are you talking about?"

He had at first thought she was talking about the ghosts and asked why she would be so happy to have found them. It was only when she dragged him down the basement steps and gave him the torch it dawned on him. John took the torch, peered in, and instinctively jumped back, his face a mask of shock and horror. Then he had done something she hadn't expected. He picked up the sledgehammer and smashed into the wall another three times until the hole was big enough to enter.

"Wait, don't go in there!"

"Why not?"

"You might touch, like, evidence or something."

"Cathy, we already know who did it. You've been trying to find him the last three weeks."

"Yeah, you might be tampering with a crime scene or something."

"Well, I'm not gonna touch them or anything. I just want to see if how they died is possible. I can't believe he bricked them up in here while they were still alive. No one could be so cruel and callous as to do that. But all that ghostly scratching we kept hearing. Shit, I checked this wall myself and found nothing. The police must have checked down here thoroughly when he killed them. How come we never found them before?"

"I don't know."

Cathy grimaced at the thought. A dizzy spell threatened to send her crashing to the floor. A wave of nausea almost had her puking, and this time it had nothing to do with pregnancy issues. The idea this man might have killed them then bricked them up alive in his own home was horrific. Left to rot and decay like vermin. That was barbaric. That kind of thing happened in the nineteenth century and before. Not now.

She thought of the two kids, especially, perhaps lying there in their own blood, their cheeks having been slit open but still clinging to life, scrabbling feebly at the wall. Then she remembered the neighbours' kid again, who at their house-warming party had ran screaming because something behind the wall had tried to grab him. All this time they had been trying to warn her, as well, to where their bodies lay; the raking at the wall, the blood on the walls, being bricked up alive herself in her dream. All this time looking for their killer and wondering where their bodies might be, and they had been there all along.

It made her shiver. It made her want to find this cruel bastard and brick him up alive somewhere he would never be found, left to die of thirst while screaming to be let free. And when John had crouched down and entered, careful not to step on anything, he had called her to show her his next discovery. At first, she hadn't wanted to, but curiosity and the need to know had overcome her. She peered in and looked to where John was pointing. Her worst fears were confirmed. Areas of the walls had long rake marks down them, dried blood where they had tried to scratch their way out—he had bricked them up in there still alive. His own wife and children.

Their tattered, bloodied clothes still clung to them in some places, the same pyjamas they wore in their ghostly form, and all three appeared to have been holding hands in their final moment—their skeletal fingers intertwined with one another. At that moment, Cathy burst into tears, overcome with grief and horror for what she had to witness, and quickly left the scene. Insisting John leave there right now, she went and grabbed her phone and called Detective Winters. He was there less than thirty minutes later.

They watched him now as he chatted with the medical examiner, who confirmed they were the remains of an adult woman and two children—one a boy, the other a girl.

"You were right, after all," said Detective Winters while the skeletons were removed.

"Yes. They'd been trying to tell us all this time, but John checked and found no signs of any recent brickwork having been done."

"My team and I checked ourselves, shortly after the disappearances were discovered. No one thought to knock the wall down and check. You're right; in this day and age, who could be so cruel as to brick up their own family?"

"They tried to claw their way out," added John. "But at least it's all over now. We've been desperate these last couple of weeks trying to figure it all out and find their killer."

Yeah, and you trying to find out if I'd been unfaithful to you. Creeping down here to try and converse with them. That was what you were most interested in.

But Cathy didn't hold a grudge against him. He had, after all, good reason to suspect. Now, fortunately, they could forget about that too.

"Well, I guess you don't have to worry about that anymore. I don't know a lot about ghosts, but I assume that once their remains have been properly buried, they'll leave you alone. And we now know they were definitely killed, so the case will be reopened and the father wanted for murder. Might help with any tips we get. Someone must know where he is."

"Oh, I forgot to tell you! I had a dream, more like a vision I think, where I saw him. He was in a large building with lots of rooms, like a hospital or a prison. In my dream, I entered his room. He was under the blanket, taunting me to find him. So I phoned the local hospital and the nearest prison but had no luck. But I'm sure he's in some kind of hospital or something similar."

"That's interesting. Under normal circumstances, I would be a little dubious about visions and dreams and so on. But given the situation, I'll have my men check into it. They may be more open to giving us information if it's a detective making the enquiries. Otherwise…"

He stopped to think for a bit. "There is, of course, Northgate Hospital for the Criminally Insane, but to end up there he would have to have been arrested first, and tried, but there have been no recent arrests that would warrant being sent there.

"There's also its sister hospital—for the Mentally Impaired, but again, same thing. One doesn't just voluntarily admit oneself to these kinds of places, unless it's urgent or the patient is a danger to themselves or others. Still, I'll check. Anyway, we'll be off. If I were you, I'd brick that place back up again soon as possible, try and get back to leading a normal life. I'll be in touch if I discover new information."

Cathy and John thanked him, then watched the whole team carry away the grisly remains. John closed the door and smiled.

"That's that, then. Now the only thing we have to scare us is your cat racing around in the middle of the night. I think a celebration is called for."

Cathy wanted to tell him she couldn't drink wine or any alcohol for the next nine months, but somehow it felt wrong telling him just yet. She was still upset they had tried to blackmail her in their desperation. That had been unnecessary and cruel. She would have helped regardless. Even so, she still needed to visit the gynaecologist for full confirmation that she was indeed pregnant. Wait until they were settled again and then she would give him the news. In the meantime, a glass of wine couldn't hurt.

A glass of wine became two and Chinese takeout by the time they went to bed, Cathy already stumbling and giggling like a little girl. They made love, both apologising afterwards for their behaviour towards each other, and were soon fast asleep. It was a few hours later Cathy grumbled in her semi-conscious state, trying to make the annoying strain in her bladder go away. It wouldn't—she needed the toilet.

Staggering slightly, she headed to the toilet, mumbling and cursing to herself for having drunk too much. She was going to pay for that tomorrow. But, as the events of the previous day returned to her, she figured a slight hangover was worth not having to listen to those ghosts haunting her, trying to ruin her life. She sat on the toilet, thinking about the poor kids and their mother and what they had been subjected to. She still couldn't believe anyone could be so cruel and twisted.

Cathy finished, flushed the toilet, and was about to head back to bed when the cat bolted past her and ran down the stairs. She chuckled. It seemed he was back to his usual self as well, running around the house at night playing whatever games cats played by themselves. When she heard him shriek at the bottom of the stairs, she went and looked, curious, imagining the thing chasing some poor little spider as though it was a juicy mouse.

She stood at the top of the stairs, watching him crouching in a ready-to-attack mode, when she heard John emerge from the bedroom, too, groaning to himself.

"Your bladder can't hold up anymore either? We're getting too old for this, you know!"

Fingers caressed the back of her neck, running a line down her back. She chuckled as she felt his lips on the nape of her neck, causing her body to tingle.

"You're not telling me you want more! In the middle of the night? You've got to go to work in the morning you know, and I have to clean up the mess in the basement."

Tingling all over caused her to tremble as his hand caressed the small of her back, slowly going lower.

"John, stop. I'm tired. I—"

She screamed as she was suddenly shoved hard in the back, her legs giving away, and she fell down the stairs. Unable to grab onto anything in time, she thudded and rolled down the stairs until she was near the bottom. Her immediate thought was of the baby inside her, but that was momentarily forgotten when she looked up and saw the three semi-translucent figures standing there, their eyes blazing like flames, scowling at her.

Chapter 30

There was a knock on the door. Cathy sat up, wincing, and instantly regretted it. Her whole body ached. She didn't think she had done any damage to the foetus inside her, which had been her primary concern, but the rest of her was sore and her legs and arms had several bruises. John had wanted to take her to hospital immediately, but she refused. Not only because she didn't think it necessary, but while there they might reveal to her, and subsequently John, she was pregnant. And she still wasn't ready to tell him yet. Especially after being pushed down the stairs, thus confirming their nightmare was not only far from over but now worse. The ghosts, rather than move on, were apparently even more desperate, prepared to harm them in the process of finding their killer.

John had been livid, shouting at the then-empty house he was gonna burn the fucking thing down, and fuck them with their threats, but eventually he had calmed down when it was clear Cathy bore no serious injuries. Another reason not to tell him yet he very well might be a father soon. A couple glasses of brandy for their nerves, and they mutually resolved once and for all what to do the next day. And now, when they were about to discuss it, after John had phoned his boss to say he couldn't make it in, someone was at the door.

"I'll get it," he said. "Don't get up."

She nodded. It was probably a salesman or something, or the postman. When he opened the door, she could hear a woman's voice, one she thought she recognised. A few seconds later, John stepped into the living room with Susanne. She didn't know whether to be glad or concerned.

"Susanne? What are you doing here?"

Susanne gave a quick smile and sat beside her. "What happened to you? You've got some nasty bruises on you. Did you fall or something?" she asked, casting a quick glance at John. The insinuation was obvious.

"I did fall, yes. Or was pushed, to be more precise."

Susanne gave another nervous, questionable glance at John. He held up his hands in a defensive posture.

"Don't look at me. I didn't do it."

Susanne stared at them both for a few seconds, clearly confused.

"You didn't answer my question," said Cathy.

"I saw on the news that the bodies had been found. I'm surprised you're not surrounded by journalists yet, although admittedly it's still early. You must be so relieved! Is it over? Have their spirits finally moved on?"

"No. That's why I'm sitting here covered in bruises. I got up last night to go to the toilet and they pushed me down the stairs."

Susanne gasped, her hand flying to her mouth. "Oh my god! That's horrible. Are you sure it was them? They have no reason for hurting you, especially now that their bodies will be in a proper resting place. I don't understand."

Cathy told her about finding the bodies and how, then the dream she had had about finally finding the father. "The only thing we don't know is what hospital he's in, assuming it was a hospital, of course. But I phoned and there was nobody fitting his description."

Susanne thought for a moment. "It still doesn't make any sense. You found their remains, and that's how they repay you? Maybe they're running out of time. If their killer isn't found quickly, they might have to move on regardless. Sometimes it happens. Sometimes spirits are given a timeframe to resolve any issues they might want closing. Or questions they want answered. A last word with loved ones. But if they don't find a way to contact that person in time, they have to leave."

"I can understand that," said Cathy, "but we don't know exactly where he is. And besides, I'm not sure you came to my home just because you saw it on the news. You said you were scared off the last time you tried to help."

A cloud seemed to drift over Susanne's face, darkening her complexion. Her eyes looked worried and marked by fear.

"You're right. That's not the reason I came. I...I had a vision myself. My daughter, Sally, came to me, said I had to carry on helping others, not be scared off by darker forces in that other realm. That it was scared of me too. So I thought of you and...what we chatted about," she said, glancing up at John again.

Cathy said nothing about the abortion and prayed Susanne didn't either. She seemed to understand from Cathy's expression, though, that the subject was still a secret between them.

"So you came to help?"

"Yes. And from what I've seen and heard so far, it was a good decision."

"Well, right now we're desperate. We thought it was all over now, so anything you can do would be highly appreciated."

"Okay, we'll start straight away. I felt a presence here as soon as I walked down the garden path."

She helped Cathy to her feet and led her to the dining room with John following, explaining it was quieter there and would make it easier to concentrate.

"You sure this is gonna work?" asked John. "I mean, it won't make them angry or something will it?"

Susanne described the process and the Soul Searchers to them both, assuring them it was perfectly okay. Cathy wasn't entirely convinced, though, from the way the medium avoided their gaze. If ghosts existed, as was now obviously the case, surely it stood to reason other entities existed as well. Perhaps not so friendly as these Soul Searchers she spoke of.

"I need you to be quiet. They will speak through me and try and tell me where this man is."

Cathy watched, clutching John's hand beside her, as Susanne leaned back in her chair and closed her eyes. Cathy immediately noticed a slight drop in temperature, an electricity in the air that made the hairs on her arms and neck prickle with static.

###

Susanne's nerves were barbed wire. Every fibre of her body pricked with fear, her heart a bomb ticking down, ready to explode in her chest. She tried to keep an image of Sally in her mind, close to her. The memory of her vision standing on that hill, feeling radiant and alive and at peace with all. Replaying Sally's words in her head over and over, telling herself she was brave, doing the right thing, that nothing could harm her anymore. But it was tough. The toughest thing she ever had to do.

She thought of the last house she had visited and the woman killing herself over the truths she had learned, the husband threatening to come for her. The silhouette at Cathy's bedroom window telling her to stay away. Or else. She banished them to the back of her mind, not completely forgotten but lingering in the background like a bad memory.

Susanne took a breath and reached out for the Soul Searchers.

As always, a fog rolled in, figures moving aimlessly along, ghostly shadows with no apparent sense of purpose. Some did, heading slowly towards the gate that would allow them to pass through this world and sleep eternally in another; others perpetually trapped, doomed to linger forever for either missing the time allotted to them before moving on or for some wrong they had committed which prevented them from sleeping forever. The Soul Searchers belonged to the first bracket. They had each been granted time to reach out to their loved ones one final time, in one case find the murderer that had left her body in a cold, wet ditch, while others had simply failed or couldn't bring themselves to be apart from friends and loved ones. And so, they had come together, an ethereal band of Samaritans, their aim to help others so they didn't fall in the same trap as they had.

She heard them before she saw them, their manic banter like a group of excited children at Christmas. Wisp-like figures swirled before her, ever closer until they were practically all merged together as one, like interwoven trails of smoke rising from a bonfire.

"*You're back!*" said one that acted as spokesman. "*We missed you, we're so glad to see you again. What brings you here?*"

Fast chatter like a band of squirrels screeching at each other ensued, making Susanne grin. She was glad to be back; she should never have left and cursed her cowardice and fear for forcing her to leave. This was her home, her real home, and nothing would make her abandon them again.

"I'm so glad to see you again! I should never have left. I'm here trying to help a couple, who in turn are trying to help a spirit family find someone. We think it's urgent, they're getting desperate, and we need your help."

She could sense John and Cathy's glare on her, probably wondering who the hell she was talking to. She could also sense another presence in the room, an aura of desperation from bodies that drifted and swirled around her, occasionally feeling the slightest touch to her skin as though being brushed with a feather. There was the faintest whiff of dirt and decay coming from them as though their spirits had lingered for too long below ground. These three spirits had yet to make the transition from Earth to a higher plane.

"*Tell me their names,*" said the Soul Searcher.

Susanne didn't need to ask Cathy now. She knew them as if they were telling her in silence to her face. She told the spirit.

"And we're looking for the one that caused their demise. He's

Soul Searchers

alive, we think in a hospital. The children's father."

She wasn't sure of the exact process but knew the Soul Searchers and all trapped souls could communicate among themselves, sending messages. This was how the Soul Searchers managed to converse with others and encourage them to move along or accept it was time to go. If anyone could find the man they were looking for, it would be them; they could communicate with a spirit who just happened to be trapped in whatever building the father was hiding in.

More nervous and excited chatter followed, Susanne unable to hear or understand exactly what was being said, but she didn't need to—they had never failed her before. While she waited for a response, something else just as urgent nagged at her conscious.

"Has...has that other returned since?"

"No. Not since the last time. All has been quiet since then."

That was good. Maybe it had returned to its lair in Hell with whatever hapless soul it had taken and wouldn't return. She felt genuinely sorry for whomever the victim may be.

After a few more minutes, the Soul Searchers were buzzing again, circling each other in apparent madness.

"We have found where this person is. He is still alive. So cruel, even now. He won't go easily. They will have to be careful."

The spirit told her where he was. A shiver rippled through her. What could he possibly have done to have ended up there indefinitely? Maybe he was hiding or he had realised the atrocious horrors he had committed and was either too much of a coward to take his own life or couldn't cope with his actions. Cathy was going to be happy knowing where he was, but at the same time, removing him from the building wasn't going to be easy.

She thanked them once again for their help and was about to leave when her heart leaped up into her throat as she gasped loudly. She tried to break the contact with the Soul Searchers, who in turn scattered and disappeared, but as much as she tried to free her mind from that place, she found herself incapable, an invisible tether impeding her from returning to her normal world.

As in her vision, the grey, murky world was replaced by utter darkness.

From somewhere that might have been the other side of the world came a deep, booming roar. Her mind felt as though it was on fire, her brain cells melting and dribbling down through the insides of her skull. She was vaguely aware of Cathy asking her if she was okay—she must have sensed something, too, perhaps Susanne's muffled whimpering.

An intense heat made Susanne sweat profusely, accentuating the idea her skull was on fire. She willed herself to return, tried to remember what Sally had said about not being afraid, that she was stronger than the thing coming towards her, but it was hard, almost impossible to think she was stronger than it while her body burned.

Her eyeballs were going to pop from their sockets, shoot out like bullets. That or melt into the hollow craters like candlewax and dribble down her cheeks. That raucous roaring was getting closer. She could smell the thing now—a million rotting corpses come back to life and heading her way.

"I told you to stay away," came its voice, crackling like thunder. "I told you what would happen. Now you have vanquished not only your life but that of your daughter, your friends. Miserable fool."

Something was tugging on her arm, no doubt Cathy, but her eyes were closed and refused to open, as did her mouth. She was in that world now, both in body and spirit, and there was nothing she could think of to break the grip the thing had on her.

"You can't hurt me," she said, "only the souls of the dead, and I'm still alive. You can't touch me yet. Go back to your foul land, leave us alone!"

Her head filled with thunder, agonising explosions as though her brain had blown up. She tried to scream, but her mouth was filled with wriggling, squirming worms, her intestines stabbed repeatedly by snakes, endless numbers of flies buzzing in her chest and head, her heart consumed by bugs, while the thing loomed over her with its multiple, burning eyes and multiple tentacles flapping as they wrapped themselves around her, tightening their grip.

The demon spewed filth at her from a gargantuan mouth that covered its face except for those thousands of eyes glowing like beacons. Her breath was becoming more and more laboured, each one more difficult than the previous. She was aware of Cathy and John slapping her face, trying to wake her from this apparent stupor, but it was too late. Sally, poor Sally, who had just tried to keep her on her chosen path, had been wrong. She was powerless to resist the onslaught, feeling herself dragged ever closer to its clutches, her head almost fully submerged in the foul creature's mouth.

She had been foolish to come here, she should have listened to her head, not her heart. Maybe it had even been that thing pretending to be Sally, tricking her into coming back to this accursed house. But if she was to die, then surely it had to be for something. If her suffering was to last for all eternity, or if she was to return under the guise of a demon herself, then the least she could do was one final act of good before she left forever.

Susanne used the last remaining ounce of strength in her body, her final breath still caught in her throat, and spat out the words Cathy needed to hear.

"Northgate mental hospital."

Then, as though enraged she had managed to reveal the secret they sought, the demon roared and clamped its mouth over her head, snapping it off as though breaking a twig from a dying tree.

In the real world, Susanne slumped to the floor, dead.

Chapter 31

Detective Winters listened intently as Cathy recounted once again everything regarding Susanne's demise. He shook his head as though disbelieving what he was hearing, and Cathy figured this was probably the case. It was still barely possible for her to believe herself. Listening to Susanne's groaning and whimpering while her body shook violently, nothing she or John did able to wake her from her paralysis. The way she had slumped to the floor in that final, terrible manner, as though something had been rattling her with invisible arms. She had no idea what had happened, exactly, only that she must have been trapped in that world somehow, very probably from the creature she talked of that had scared her away the first time. At first, she had believed Susanne was in some kind of unconscious state, her energy spent from spending her time there, but after a few minutes, and when John had checked her pulse and found none, she knew the tragic truth. An ambulance arrived within minutes, then she phoned the detective once Susanne's body had been removed and she had answered police questions.

Cathy wiped her eyes once she finished and took another sip of wine, feeling guilty about it but needing it at the same time. The anxiety and spouts of nausea were almost overwhelming now. It made her wonder how her baby was feeling down there. Could he sense all this horror that had occurred only a short time ago? John took her hand and clutched it, then kissed her forehead. Poor guy. After everything she had put him through, he still didn't know he was going to be a father. That knowledge would not be long in coming, though. As soon as this was over. Definitely.

"I'm very sorry to hear about her demise, but tragic as it is, I'm more interested right now in what she said to you just before she died. I just got off the phone to the Director of Northgate Hospital. She's willing to talk to us further, help solve this case once and for all. I'm going there right now, in fact. Normally, I doubt you would be allowed to accompany me inside, but if we tell them you can identify the person, that should be enough.

"So, you coming?"

As much as she felt intense despair for Susanne's demise, the need to end this horror overwhelmed it. As soon as the detective said he was going there right now and she could come along, her expression of dismay was replaced by one of hope and relief. She felt guilty for it but promised herself she would regularly visit Susanne's grave and leave fresh flowers, keep her in her prayers. It was the least she could do.

She jumped up, forgetting about her still-bruised body and aches and pains.

"I guess you should stay here, John," she said. "They won't let both of us in."

"Okay, but just make sure you catch the son of a bitch."

"I promise."

She kissed him and left with Detective Winters, her heart now aching not with grief but an adrenaline-fuelled relief.

On the outside, Northgate Hospital for the Mentally Impaired looked like any normal hospital except for the bars set in place on the third floor windows, giving it an ominous, dangerous appearance. She knew nothing about the hospital except from what the detective had told her on the way. The majority of patients there entered and left voluntarily, receiving treatment for illnesses such as schizophrenia, depression, or anxiety issues. The third floor was reserved for more dangerous patients, those for whom there was no cure or medication and who may present a danger to themselves and others. If Alex Hamshore was anywhere, he was up there, perhaps having booked himself in for reasons she could only guess. Now that she thought about the vision she had had, the barred windows, padded walls, and psychotic screaming coming from other rooms, she agreed this was where he would be.

She felt dizzy as they walked down the long path towards the entrance. She thought this day would never come and that not only might she lose her husband, after being pushed down the stairs she might lose the baby too. And yet, at the same time, coming face to face with this monster, for real and not in some dream or vision, terrified her. What if he attacked them and escaped? Detective Winters was a large man, well-built, but didn't they say mad men had the strength of ten? He had been capable of cutting the bodies of his own family then bricking them up in the basement—that meant he was capable of literally anything. But she guessed for those on the top ward, there would be extra security in the event of such an occurrence, so she tried to keep calm, taking deep breaths. But the desire to vomit would not go away.

The detective patted her on the back reassuringly. "It'll be all right. If he's here, we'll find and arrest him."

They stepped into the hospital and headed straight to reception. A young woman sat there, busy typing. He produced his badge and told her they wanted to speak to the director. The receptionist phoned someone and told them to wait. It might have only been a few seconds, but it felt an eternity.

A stern, serious-looking middle-aged woman finally came to meet them. Cathy thought she might often be mistaken for a man with her big build, cropped, grey hair, and very little, if any, makeup. Both rose to greet her, and after the detective explained what they were there for, she agreed and took them up the lift to the top floor.

"We're looking for someone who may have been here a while, admitted himself, and probably has had no visitors. I expect him to be quite delusional, possibly cruel, violent even towards others. He would be going under a false name as well."

"We do have someone who may match that description. A man, Richard Darwin, admitted himself a year ago saying he was suffering from chronic hallucinations. Violent ones, and that he had attacked someone but couldn't remember doing it. He awoke in an alley with someone's blood on his jacket. He told us he had no next of kin, no family. After a while we thought he was getting better, but when we reduced his medication, he attacked another patient, nearly killing them in the process. He's had to be kept in solitary since then, only allowed out to exercise when accompanied by three orderlies. I'm guessing this might be your man."

Cathy and the detective cast knowing glances at each other. Yes, it did indeed seem like their man.

"Take us to him, please. Cathy here needs to identify him. He's wanted for a series of brutal murders."

"Follow me, then," she said, not looking at all happy Cathy was going to accompany them.

They entered a lift and headed to the third floor. They stepped outside and found themselves at another reception, a girl typing and two burly orderlies chatting. They both lost the grins on their faces when they saw their boss.

"I'd like you to take us to Richard Darwin, please. Be prepared for anything. He may try and escape."

The two orderlies stood to attention, sharing looks of confusion but stretching their muscles at the same time. The director, Jackie, led them to a thick, metallic door and unlocked it, opening it onto a long ward reminiscent of a prison. Each cell had a small window set in the middle, iron bars fixed so employees could see in before opening the doors.

Ripples of fear and unease made Cathy shudder as she took in the sight, exactly as she had seen in her dream, an intense case of deja vu. Banging and wailing came from several of the cells, while from others came a creepy sobbing like a child lost and afraid. But Jackie and the orderlies ignored them completely, sometimes banging on doors themselves and telling the patients to be quiet. Some replied by screaming obscenities at them, trying to spit between the thick bars, inviting both Jackie and Cathy into their cells to perform some unspeakable act upon them. Cathy did her best not to show how scared she was, focusing straight ahead, keeping close to the detective. They stopped right where she knew they would, at the bottom of the ward, fourth cell down on the right, as though she was a regular to this accursed hospital.

She was struggling to breathe, having to force deep breaths, and this immediately made her think of the baby growing inside. What stress was she putting on him right now?

An orderly peered through the small opening and nodded. "He's asleep in bed."

The detective indicated for Cathy to look in, see if she could recognise him from outside, yet when she looked, all she could see was the back of his head. She remembered she hadn't actually seen him in that dream, only heard his gruff voice, and when she had been bricked up in the basement, she could recall nothing except his grim eyes.

She shrugged and told him.

"All right, open the door," ordered Winters.

The guard unlocked it, and both guards stepped in first.

"Darwin, someone here to see you. Wake up," said one in a gruff voice. He prodded him with his arm then stepped back. The man under the blanket, just as he was in Cathy's dream, grunted and rolled over.

"I don't wanna see anyone, leave me alone."

"Get up, I said."

The man grunted again, cursing under his bed, and threw back the blanket. He sat up. Cathy gasped, clapping a hand to her mouth.

It was him.

She didn't recognise any of his features, the mop of greasy, brown hair, taut, stretched skin, or the scruffy beard on his face. He might have been some poor man with mental issues, no different to anyone else, totally unremarkable. Except for his eyes. They glared accusingly, suspiciously, at the five people staring back at him, and immediately Cathy was taken back to the night of her dream, trapped behind a brick wall, those piercing eyes taunting her before he placed the last brick. She shuddered and quickly stepped back out.

"Recognise him?" asked Winters.

She simply nodded, unable to speak for fear of throwing up.

"All right. Take deep breaths. Jackie, it's him."

She nodded while Winters moved to the side of the bed, towering over him. "Ricard Darwin is it?"

"Yeah. Whaddaya want?"

"Or perhaps I should say Alex Hamshore. Recognise that name?"

As Cathy peered once more from behind the door, she saw a look of defeat on his face. Brief, but just enough for her to know what he was thinking—he had been caught.

"Dunno what you're talkin' about. Never 'eard of 'im."

"That so. Well, your fingerprints will tell us down at the station if it's you or not, but for now I'm arresting you for the murders of your wife and two children."

Cathy barely heard the detective read the rest of his rights while telling him to get dressed. She was too busy crying, not believing they had finally found him. She was about to say he should also be arrested for the murder of Susanne, because inadvertently he had killed her as well, but it was enough this was finally over.

The two orderlies crowded the man in case he attempted to escape, but he simply rose and allowed his hands to be cuffed behind his back. The detective gave Cathy a quick, reassuring smile as he dragged him from the cell.

In his car, Winters handcuffed Alex to a metal bar on the back of his own seat then slammed the door shut.

Cathy wiped her eyes, not wanting to give him the satisfaction of seeing her crying. She wanted to say something to him, ask him how he could be so evil as to brick up his own family, tell him how she had found out where he was. But right now she was too tired, her head too riddled with emotions to say it. Winters didn't seem to have the same problem though.

"Tell me, how did you feel when you bricked them up? Could you hear your children's screaming, begging to be let out? Were they still alive after being stabbed?"

He said nothing.

"Do you want to know how we found you? You thought you were being clever, that you'd got away with it, didn't you? Well, you're not going to believe how we discovered where you were. But you're going to find out."

Cathy turned and looked at the detective, not quite sure if she had heard him right. He smiled at her and said no more, but Cathy got a glimpse into his thinking when they drove down her street and stopped outside her house. He parked the car, stepped out, and unlocked Alex from the bar he was attached to before dragging him out, hard enough he almost went sprawling on the ground.

"Thought you was going to go to prison, did you? Well, I think there are some people who'd like to meet you first. Right, Cathy?"

Still too dumbfounded to answer, she nodded.

"What you gonna do?" demanded Alex. "Gonna beat me up? Kill me? Guess what, I don't give a shit."

"Good to hear."

He dragged him down the garden path and waited for Cathy to open the door. As she did so, John saw them and came running then stopped, a look of utter confusion on his face when he saw the handcuffed man.

"Is that him? You found him?"

"Yes, it is. We believe so, anyway. We'll soon find out, I think."

The second Alex was pushed inside, the whole house seemed to emit a resounding groan, as though shaking on its foundations or breathing a sigh of relief. Despite the hall light being on, the area darkened. The basement door creaked open. Alex looked wildly around, perhaps sensing for the first time something was wrong.

The cat, sitting at the top of the stairs, hissed and bolted. The air became thicker, making it hard to breath, as though they were stuck in a very small room with no circulation of oxygen, hot and stuffy. The basement door slammed shut and then back open against the wall.

"I guess we should go down there," said Winters. He dragged Alex to the top of the stairs and forced him down the steps, John and Cathy behind.

Immediately, from all around them came the sounds of crying, moaning, and wailing. Shadows darted back and forth, too fast to determine their identities, but Cathy didn't need to see them to know. She gripped John's hand, who held her close as they remained halfway down the stairs.

"Remember this, Alex?" asked Winters. "That's the hole we made where we found their skeletons. They'd clawed their fingernails off. You can still see the smears of blood as your kids and wife tried frantically to claw their way out. How'd you feel about that?"

Again he said nothing but glanced around the room, following shadows, looking both terrified and confused.

The sobbing abruptly stopped, followed by what might have been a howl of anguish. Brick dust fell from the large gap in the wall, a scraping sound came from within, something dragging itself along the floor. Then three shadows appeared from the hidden room and slowly stepped out, walking straight through the wall. Alex grunted.

He tried to back away, but Winters held him firmly. The three semi-translucent shapes of the mother and her children stepped into view, their faces cut open, blood running down their torn, filthy pyjamas, mouths twisted into sneers, holding out their arms showing bloodied stubs for fingers.

"Is this him?" asked Winters, who didn't seem the slightest bit unnerved to be confronted by three ghosts. Alex, though, was shaking his head in disbelief, mumbling incoherencies to himself.

As if in answer, all three ghosts' mouths opened impossibly wide, and a deafening, piercing scream came from them, causing Cathy to cover her ears. The walls shook, more dust falling from the gap in the wall. The lightbulb swung violently back and forth like a pendulum, causing more eerie shadows to decorate the rest of the basement.

"They've been waiting for you, Alex. Wanted to say their goodbyes, I believe. I wonder why?" He threw him towards the spirits.

Alex yelped and tried to run but suddenly found himself paralysed in midturn, one leg in the air as he tried to sprint. They watched in awe as his back arched as though pushed, and he was dragged towards them, grimacing, until he was inches from them. They ran their hands over his face as though caressing him, but the look on their faces suggested anything other than joy. Blood seeped from between the bricks again as the bloodied stubs of the two children picked and pulled at the flesh on Alex's face. He tried to scream, yet a hand covered his mouth as he was slowly forced to the floor, lying there immobile. Cathy noticed that not once did he even attempt to apologise for what he had done.

The wall behind them began to shake violently. Bricks came loose as the spirits stood over Alex, their expressions now void of any emotion. Perhaps they were just tired or relieved they could finally see justice done. Cathy could never forgive them for what they had put her through, but now, seeing their killer grovelling beneath them, she could at least understand their intentions. Maybe Susanne had been right; they were on a timeframe and urgency had forced them to take drastic measures.

Huge cracks appeared in the wall, stretching out across the ceiling as it loosened. A brick fell and landed on Alex's leg, then another. At first, Cathy assumed it to be coincidence, but within a few seconds it became clear it was nothing of the kind. Alex screamed and grimaced with each thud of the bricks on his body; he was rapidly being covered up by them.

A brick landed on his face, hitting him directly on the nose. Blood gushed into his screaming mouth. Another hit him squarely on the cheek, then in the eye. It was obvious he was trying to move, yet with his arms handcuffed behind his back, every time he tried to squirm out of the way he was forced onto his back again.

It was as if someone was physically removing the bricks from the wall. They squeezed themselves out and were flung at Alex's body and face. The gap Cathy had made was now big enough for her and John to walk through side by side. And still they rained down on top of him, splitting his nose and mouth. In a short space of time, he was barely visible anymore. A mound of bricks covered him, his blood seeping out from the sides as his screams became weak moans and muffled groans. Then they watched, amazed, as a brick released itself from a wall that was now barely there and hovered over Alex. It hung in the air for a few seconds, like some alien, wingless creature, then flew down and smashed Alex so hard on the forehead the brick exploded upon contact, sending bits flying everywhere. Alex shook for a few seconds, as though having a fit, and was silent. The rest of the wall tumbled down and covered him completely.

The ghosts turned to face the detective, then John and Cathy, before turning around and walking away, fading as they left. The last they heard or saw was a faint wailing that might have been the baby they had heard so many times already or Alex's last breath. The room went silent. For the first time since they moved in, the cat dared to peer its head into the basement to see what the fuss was all about.

The silence lasted for another couple of minutes, until Detective Winters turned to face them. "I don't believe in seeking one's own justice, the world would be chaos, but in this instance, I think prison would have been too good for him. I don't know if he's dead or not, and I don't care, but I'm going to call it in and say he escaped when I came to drop you off home. We managed to stop him, and the wall fell on top of him during the struggle. Nothing more will come of it—my colleagues and boss will just be glad to have finally caught him, so you might want to have something to drink before they come. For the nerves. There will probably be a lot of questions anyway.

"As for me, I think I'm going to start going to church more often. Not that I've got a lot to answer for, but seems like a good idea. You ready for this?"

John wrapped an arm around Cathy and nodded. Cathy nodded, too, her hand rubbing absently at her belly. She didn't feel so nauseated now, a great weight removed from her body and soul. She decided she would tell John tonight she might be pregnant. She also thought that if it was a girl, she might name her Susanne.

###

Susanne was four years old already. Cathy couldn't believe how fast she grew. She was already speaking with amazing proficiency and acted like a girl two or three years older. Rarely did she cry, not even when she fell over and hurt herself. In fact, Cathy couldn't remember the last time she had heard her cry. Both she and John congratulated themselves on a job well done, and every night when Cathy put Susanne to bed, it was she that had tears of joy running down her cheeks. Even the birth had been virtually painless, Susanne sliding out quickly and easily, and even then she had needed to be smacked by the nurse to get her to cry. She was perfect.

Detective Winters, who had since become a godfather to Susanne, had been right about the questions two years ago; the other investigators had been more relieved the case could be closed. Alex had been buried in an unmarked grave, and no one had come to his funeral. That night, Cathy revealed her secret, apologising for her recent behaviour but telling him she had another reason, not just being haunted by three vengeful spirits. John had cried with delight when she told him the news.

Now, nearly five years later, they laughed about the events with the spirits. They laughed at the things they had said to each other, the way they had screamed in the middle of the night at seeing shadowy figures, Cathy screaming when she awoke from another nightmare. But they didn't laugh about the two dead children and their mother; instead, they visited their graves regularly to leave flowers. Neither John nor Cathy saw their spirits again, and John never found out about the abortion. Things were very good once more.

Except, not quite.

The first thing they found unusual was that Sparky—ghosts aside—who was normally very friendly around others, be it humans or kids, was acting very odd. On that fateful day when the neighbours' kid had come to their house, Sparky had allowed the kid to pick him up and stroke him before dashing off. But when Cathy had come home with Susanne wrapped up in a warm bundle, he had hissed and bolted. They had discussed that sometimes dogs got jealous, but cats? Cats didn't give a shit about such irrelevancies. He was the boss no matter who came into their home.

And he refused to go anywhere near her. When Cathy picked him up and got anywhere close to Susanne, whether it was in her cot or playing on the floor, he nearly scratched Cathy's eyes out trying to break free from her grasp. John and Cathy laughed, saying he was jealous and would have to get used to it. Fives years later, they didn't laugh anymore. Far from it, because six months ago, when Susanne was playing on the living room floor, the cat had taken a swipe at her, leaving a fine cut across her cheek. Susanne screamed, and Cathy gasped in shock. Since then, she made damn sure she kept an eye on the cat whenever Susanne was alone.

And then there was the way Susanne would giggle at nothing, stare up at the ceiling just as the cat had done all that time ago, that made Cathy shiver with unease.

"What is it, honey? What do you see? What are you giggling at?"

But Susanne refused to answer, as if it was some secret only she could know about, and it made Cathy extremely nervous. Despite not a single incident in the house since that time, no fleeing shadows, the only wailing belonging to Susanne as she played or sung alone, she still couldn't shake off the thought they might come back.

John told her it had been an extremely stressful time and would inevitably take a while for all the emotional scars to heal. But he was at the office all day, close to receiving a promotion already, so was hardly around. And when he was, it didn't take long for him to fall asleep on the sofa. So more often than not, it left her alone with just her daughter and a freaked-out cat to contend with.

Then there were issues at daycare, regularly getting into fights with other kids. On one occasion, Cathy had been called in because Susanne called another girl a bitch and tugged hard on her hair, causing the girl to scream in shock and pain. When asked about it, Cathy was pretty sure she caught a quick, sly grin from Susanne before she hung her head in fake shame.

But of all the things that bothered Cathy about her daughter, what she was doing right now bothered her the most. She had recently taken to drawing with crayons, and at first they had been the typical preschooler scribbles—Mum and Dad, the house, birds and animals—but now they had taken a darker, more sinister turn. She looked cute and cuddly right now with her brow furrowed and the tip of her tongue poking out as though concentrating extremely hard on her latest creation, but she had been doing the same thing when she proudly presented her mother a drawing of the cat.

Minus its head, which lay beside it in a pool of blood.

Now she was drawing a picture of three figures. Cathy couldn't quite figure out who they were supposed to be. Susanne had coloured the whole piece of paper in a light grey, and there were dark smudges like shadows everywhere, vaguely human shaped. What she could tell was that of the three figures, two were smaller than the other, leading her to assume they were children. They were blurry with no discernible features, and Cathy got the impression it was meant to be this way—secretive, obscure figures hiding in a thick fog.

Then Susanne grabbed her black crayon and drew something that made Cathy grimace. It looked like some kind of octopus with flailing tentacles, something resembling claws on the end of each one. With her red crayon she drew two bright circles in the middle of its head, like flames, then long, exaggerated pointed teeth with her white crayon. It was when Susanne drew two more figures directly in front of the octopus thing, red slits across their throats, that Cathy made her daughter stop.

"What are you drawing, babe? That looks nasty."

"It's you and Dad in front of my friend. The one I speak to each night. He says he's coming to visit us soon. Won't that be fun, Mummy?!"

The End

Also by Justin Boote

Short Story Collections:

Love Wanes, Fear is Forever
Love Wanes, Fear is Forever: Volume 2
Love Wanes, Fear is Forever: Volume 3

Novels:

Serial
Combustion
Chasing Ghosts
Carnivore: Book 1 of The Ghosts of Northgate trilogy
The Ghosts of Northgate: Book 2 of The Ghosts of Northgate trilogy
A Mad World: Book 3 of The Ghosts of Northgate trilogy
The End of Things as He Knew Them (with Angel Van Atta)

The Undead Possession Series –
Book 1: Infestation
Book 2: Resurrection
Book 3: Corruption
Book 4: Legion
Book 5: Resurgence

From Wicked House Publishers
In Grandma's Room (a YA horror novel)

Short stories available on Godless
Badass
Grandmother Drinks Blood
If Flies Could Fart
A Question of Possession

Also by J. Boote (extreme horror)

Man's Best Friend
Love You To Bits
Buried

The Monsters Series:

They are all Monsters
Am I a Monster?
Born or Bred (Pigs and Monsters)

Made in United States
Orlando, FL
10 April 2024

45677305R00093